D0563531

The Man Who
Corrupted Heaven

The Man Who
Corrupted Heaven

Andrew Hood

Copyright © 2019 by Andrew Hood
All rights reserved.

Peregrino Press
De Pere, WI

This book is dedicated to

My wife
Elizabeth

And our children
Lynton, Harrison & Rose

I love you all,
Forever

Acknowledgments

———•———

IT HAS TAKEN ME OVER two years to write, rewrite and edit this book. So many people have contributed to it over that time, and it is impossible list them all, but I will do my best to capture a few.

First and foremost, I need to acknowledge the love and support that I have received from my wife Liz. Everything that I am and that is good in my life all started from the moment I met you, my love. Thank you!

Next, I need to thank and acknowledge my beautiful children Lynton, Harrison and Rose, my mother Lill and my father Ed. I am so lucky to be surrounded by the love of all of you, and I am grateful for it every day.

Given that none of you had read a single word of this book for the first two years of its creation, your support is even more impactful. You all have so much faith in me that it makes everything I do easier.

I would also like to thank Rosie McCaffrey and Joanne Shwed who did an amazing job developmental editing and copyediting this book and Randy Peyser from Author One Stop for all her guidance through the process.

We all have people in our lives who make an impact. These

people see through the painted-on smile and care what is really going on underneath. Whether they are family, friends, work colleagues or even relative strangers, they are important to us. Without them, the sun would not shine as brightly. To the people who support me and make my life better, I thank you!

Contents

Follow the Money

——•——

I T IS OFTEN SAID THAT you come into this world with nothing and leave it the same way. Isaac McGlynn, however,
was determined to prove this adage wrong.

After dedicating himself to the accumulation of money,
Isaac finally had enough to satisfy his every desire. His
clothes, which were delivered to him weekly, had been
designed specifically for his tall but lean stature and pale skin
tone. His hair was the color of walnuts, and his eyes burned
with an undeniable intensity. With exclusive ocean-view
property, expensive cars, luxury boats and private planes,
he had made his list and checked it twice. It was all there,
but having it all — and the power it brought him — was
not enough. He wanted to take some of it with him from
this world to the next. After all, why should a man who had
succeeded in one lifetime not enjoy the spoils into the next?

Every time Isaac thought about all that he would lose on
his deathbed, his anger burned like a solar flare. It seemed
that not only would death conquer him, it would also steal
from him.

He had spent millions of dollars trying to prolong his
demise, but now the cancer was eating him from the inside

and the doctors were telling him that his time on the earth was nearly done. His candle had burnt too fast, and soon all that remained would be a final wave of smoke curling through the air.

* * *

Just back from the hospital, Isaac headed for his office. There was no point in going home. Apart from the minimal staff to maintain his city penthouse, there was no one waiting for him there. There was also not a single person in the world who was anxiously waiting for news of his health because he had told no one. That needed to change.

* * *

"I don't need much space," he had said to his agent, "but it needs to be the absolute best. Top floor, city view. It needs to scream money."

That is what he got.

Every day, hundreds of millions of dollars of other people's money were traded on their behalf with only one true winner: Isaac McGlynn. Now, back at his mahogany desk, Isaac placed his hands, palms down, against the wood to brace himself one last time.

"Susan!"

While he waited for his assistant, he collected all the paperwork from his desk into a single pile and promptly dropped it indiscriminately into the first drawer that he could reach. He had considered putting it in the trash but caught himself. None of it seemed to matter to him anymore, but it might to others.

He was not accustomed to waiting and almost repeated his command when Susan finally arrived at his door. She had been patting herself down, obviously wanting to present well.

"Yes, Isaac?"

Isaac allowed himself a moment to remember the first time Susan had entered his office. It gave him a wave of awe, lust and even a little self-loathing, all in one delicious, emotional meal. Something about his current situation gave him a new view of the world. It was now showing him a glimpse, behind the sexual realm, that he had never noticed before.

Susan was the most beautiful — and accommodating — personal assistant that money could buy. Without fully understanding why, he had known within the first 10 minutes of meeting her that he wanted her close until he could break her spell over him. They had worked through her employment contract with no other party present. It was a test. If she followed his every command and agreed to his specific job description for a period of five years, he would ensure that she would never have to work again. She would be a rich woman by most normal standards but still a mere minnow to his own.

There was no task or whim that Susan would not satisfy for Isaac — professionally, personally or even sexually. Once she had even procured others for Isaac when he had decided he wanted "a little variety."

He had never married, but he was still a man with needs, and what better way to meet those needs than with a simple, unemotional transaction? After all, that is how his world evolved: one transaction after another.

"Pay a little, get what you need from a professional, and owe nothing afterward."

Relationships, on the other hand, required huge investments in time, attention and money. The risks were high and the rewards too inconsistent for his liking. "Risk was for suckers," he had been known to say, but of course he never said these words to any of his customers. He had profited handsomely from their risks.

He considered what inappropriate request he might make of Susan but instead snapped himself back to the task at hand.

"Clear my day, and then get John and one of my lawyers in here right away. I need to make a will. Actually, ask the agency to send over Steven Holloway. He's never done any legal work for us, but I think he'll be suitable and very keen for this task when I explain what's in it for him."

"Yes, sir," Susan replied. She turned to retreat and then paused. With a considered smile, she added, "I hope you won't forget about me in that will of yours. Should I perhaps relieve a little of that tension first so you can think more clearly?"

"No, thank you, Susan. I'll keep my tension for now," he answered before waving her away.

* * *

The pain spreading across his stomach was toxic but would not slow him down today. Within 15 minutes, Isaac had the requested people around him, waiting for his command. This outcome was impressive given that his lawyers' offices were more than 20 minutes away.

He turned first to his business partner — John Hannebery, his lieutenant and the only man he had ever trusted in business or in life. John was an unkept hulk of a man who favored his right side and protected his left like a boxer with a bad liver. They had met as children and had bonded for their mutual safety. John's special place in Isaac's life was based on his willingness to serve Isaac unquestionably, even if it got him into trouble.

Isaac had been considering this next step for the last four weeks.

"John, I have made you a rich man, but now I'm about to take you to another level. I hope you're ready for it."

John licked his lips and nodded slowly. Isaac was pleased that he had not spoken. Greed always had a way of telling the smart when to keep their mouth shut and the stupid when to talk.

Isaac set the ground rules and began. "Nothing I am about to say will leave this office. You ..." He pointed to Steven Holloway who, at Isaac's request, had been appointed by the agency.

Steven had the look of a man whose mind was always else-where and who never quite understood how to gracefully maneuver the body he was given.

"Yes?" Steven asked timidly.

"I would like you to draw up a will for me. Can you do that?"

"Well, it isn't my specialty but, yes, I can try."

This response was not enough for Isaac. It had to be rock solid. "I pay a lot of money for people who can make things happen. I don't want triers. Can you *do* it? Yes or no? If you can, I will make it very worth your while, but it will need to be bulletproof!"

Steven's demeanor changed instantly. "Yes! Yes, I can do it."

Isaac sized him up and decided that he would be acceptable.

He turned to Susan. "Please make one of the desks near you available for Steven. He will not be making any copies or taking any of his own paperwork out of this office once we start the process. That sanction will last to the very end when I finally sign the contract."

"Understood," she replied. Susan either hadn't found the request unusual or was simply accustomed to doing whatever her boss instructed.

The lawyer, summonsed by a rich man whom he had never seen before, looked like an animal suddenly trapped in a cage. Steven ran his fingers through his thinning, brown-gray hair and smothered the sweat that was pushing its way to the surface of his temples. "I'm not sure I can stay here all day. I may need to use the resources back at the ..."

Isaac cut him off. "Steven, before you say another word, let me put this into perspective for you. If you stay here and follow my instructions exactly, I will pay you $1 million in cash. That money is less than 100 feet from this desk, although you could search for a week and never find it. Nobody other than the people in this room will ever know you have it. Not even that wife and three children of yours. And all those gambling debts — gone! Nobody ever needs to know." Isaac could see that he had already caught the man off guard. "I'm a rich man, Steven Holloway. I make it my business to always know who I am working with."

The lawyer seemed suddenly unsure what to do with his hands. Then, a little too quickly, he said, "Yes. Sure. I'm in."

"Good. Now let's get down to business." Then, as if he were ordering lunch, Isaac announced, "I'm dying. And I want to make a secret will. So secret in fact, that death himself won't even know about it."

John looked shocked, but it was unclear if his look was about Isaac's mortality or the fact that his meal ticket was about to expire. "*Dying?* What are you *talking* about? Why I didn't know about this?"

"I'm sorry, old friend. I needed to exhaust all options before telling anyone," Isaac replied. "I didn't want the business to suffer."

Now it was Susan's turn to ask a question. "How long have you got? You have been looking unwell, but I always thought it was just temporary."

Isaac studied her face. She seemed genuinely sad for him. For the first time in many years, he felt sorry for another human being besides John. Perhaps she had enjoyed some of his company after all. He had, in a way, liberated this young woman. He was quite sure that even two years before had he hired her, she would not have performed any of the special daily tasks he requested of her. Now, when required, she commanded a room of powerful men on his behalf. Perhaps he could have formed a relationship with the opposite sex after all, and it would never have been anyone other than this particular woman.

"Not long," Isaac answered. "One, maybe two months if I push it. Don't worry though. I have no intention of dragging it out." Isaac turned to the lawyer. "I am about to give you a copy of a personal contract signed by myself and this beautiful woman. You are to take the payout figure from the document and triple it."

Susan gasped. "*What?* No, Isaac. You don't need to do that. It's already too much. I'm not worth that."

Isaac objected. "Oh, but you are, Susan. You are worth that

and much more. It is me who has cheapened you through that damn contract." He turned again to the lawyer. "As you read the details in this contract, Steven, you may be surprised by how candid we have been. If you lift so much as one judgmental eyebrow in this woman's direction, not only will our deal be off, but I will ensure that you never work outside of an ice-cream stand again. Is that understood?"

"Understood."

"Good. You two will need to work together, for the short term anyway. Simply take what's there, make it completely respectable, and triple the figure." He turned back to Susan. "Are you okay with this? I did promise you that no one would ever see it, but I think we are in safe hands here."

Susan had a tear in the corner of her eye. "I am not ashamed of our arrangement."

Isaac was a little surprised by her response. "No, the shame should be all mine for suggesting it in the first place." There was so much more about this woman that he would have liked to discover if there was time.

Isaac turned to John. "Now, to make sure that you're taken care of, I want you to try and extend as many customer contracts as you can in the next thirty days. When I'm gone, you can expect twenty-five percent of the customers to leave if they aren't already locked in. Before you give me that indignant look of yours, it's not personal. It's simply that you won't have the same leverage as I do. Just assure them that any secrets held by me, I took with me. I have no interest in ruining anyone from beyond the grave. If you make sure they know that, you might keep a few on the books.

"Also, you might want to remind them that I may have been a little underhanded in getting some of them onto our books, but I still made them rich. I turned their $50,000 into a quarter of a million within the first twelve months of business. Whenever I saw their sour fucking faces, I just wanted to shove dollar bills up their noses. The end always justified the means. *Always!* And, if they don't like it, tell them that they can give all the money back and fuck off."

John nodded. "You seem to have this all planned out."

"This is the easy part. I've had a few weeks to think about it. Before I get to the complicated stuff, though, I need to know one thing from you both." Isaac paused as a small wave of emotion threatened to break his composure. "Outside of the two of you, I don't care for people. And, as a result, nobody really cares for me."

John started to interject, but Isaac silenced him once again with a wave of his hand. "Sure, they may respect me, John but that's not the point. Regardless of what I feel for them, I do care about you two. I need to know that you are taken care of. Are you both happy with what I have given you? Is there anything else you want before this conversation takes a turn?"

Susan spoke first. "You've given me so much already. More than I deserve. And you could keep it all if it meant that I could keep you alive. However, if you're going to die anyway, it would be a shame to see that beautiful, blue Aston Martin go to waste," she said with a seductive smile.

John scoffed. "Oh, Susan, you hussy! You beat me to it. I'll have the Ferrari."

For the next twenty minutes, they haggled over some of Isaac's prized possessions like children dividing a bag of candy. Every time an item was decided, Isaac would nod to Steven, and the lawyer would make note of the allocation on his legal pad. This was exactly the way Isaac wanted the conversation to go. For the first time in his life, he felt like Santa Claus. There was even laughter as they forgot what had gotten them to the bargaining table in the first place.

Isaac felt a strange sense of warmth spread through his body. And, for the first time in weeks, the ever-present pain left. However, even though he was being granted a brief reprieve, he knew that it would soon be back.

Negotiating Death

ISAAC HAD ASKED SUSAN TO order them lunch and have it delivered to the office. He had only eaten a quarter of his exotic sandwich, but the morning's discussions had fueled the appetites of the others. They had each eaten their sandwich and the rest of his, which seemed to harbor a secret ingredient designed for the rich to make the mundane amazing. Now, two hours after they had first started their meeting, and with only a few sandwiches of unknown character left, it was time to get back down to business.

Susan broke the silence when she suddenly erupted through a mouthful of half-eaten food, "My god. I can't *believe* it! I forgot to ask. What do you have? What are you dying from?"

Isaac laughed. Rather than be insulted, he was a little proud. It was not directly important after all. They had all been focused when money was on the line, and now it was time for some background information. He had never discussed his illness with anyone other than his doctor, so he wasn't immediately sure which words to choose or how to approach it.

He decided to start with the facts. "I have pancreatic cancer. It's hard to detect. Usually by the time you find it, you have little time left to act. In my case, I have almost none."

"Is that why you haven't been eating lately?" John asked.

"You don't know the half of it, but yes, that's the reason I haven't been eating. There's a raft of other symptoms I've tried to hide from you both." Isaac paused, caught in a thought, and then shook himself free. "Anyway, while I haven't been eating food, the cancer has been eating away at me for a while. It looks like the little bastard has hollowed the life right out of me." Isaac pushed away the sandwich and also lost his taste for the subject. "Steven, do you have everything that we've discussed this morning written down or recorded?"

The lawyer pushed away his own plate, taking the cue that lunch was finished. He grabbed his pad and took a quick look at his notes. "Yes. I think I have everything."

"Not yet, you don't," Isaac replied. "You have this morning only. Take a new page and get ready. We're going to discuss my death."

"Don't you mean funeral?" Susan asked.

"No. I mean my death."

Confusion hung in the air as Isaac took a moment to consider his words. If he didn't say them right, he would ramble. At this moment, he needed to be clear. He studied his hands, which had always been his best method to focus his mind.

"I'll be honest," Isaac continued. "I really don't care if there is no funeral after I'm gone. Sure, I'm a rich man, and they will come out of the woodwork to show their support or stake their claim. Hell, some will come just to confirm for themselves that I am actually dead. I ask you two," he said, pointing to John and Susan. "Will there be one honest tear shed among them?"

"To hell with them," Susan replied. "I'll cry." Her eyes were already holding back the flood.

Isaac grabbed her hand. It was the first time he had ever touched her tenderly. "Then let's cry together. I'm sure that, if I try hard enough, I might be able to remember how to do it. But my pride makes no demand for a funeral. John, you decide if a funeral will help you in any way with the business. If it will, go for it. If not, kill it ... so to speak."

Isaac turned back to Steven. "Let John be your guide on my funeral. I don't want to be involved in the details. My death, on the other hand, needs to be precisely planned. You see, I have spent my lifetime building my fortune, and I'll be damned if I let death take it all from me."

John looked concerned. "But, Isaac, you *can't* take it with you. Susan and I already have enough. What do you plan to do with the rest of it?"

Isaac replied through gritted teeth, "I *can* take it with me, and I will! I'll get to that in a minute." He pulled a notebook from his desk drawer and opened it to a page full of notes. "We are going to set the date of my death to the 30th of October, exactly four weeks away. The doctor says that I have six weeks, but I'm determined to seal my own fate. Another thing that death won't take from me is choice. We are going to work backwards from this date on a 'steps to death' plan.

Susan looked horrified. "Steps to death?"

"That's right. Each week between now and then, you are going to donate $1 million of my money to each of the top two world religions: Catholicism and Islam. Spread it around. I'm playing the numbers game. I don't care which one is right. I just want to grease the palms of the gods before I get there in the odd chance that they exist." After a pause, he continued. "Oh, John, make sure that one specific church — and you and I know all too well which one it is — does not get a single cent. If they have a god, he can go screw himself."

John nodded, understanding but stunned. "I'm not sure that's the way it works, Isaac. You can't buy your way into heaven."

"I'm not. I'm advertising."

"Advertising what?"

"My coming arrival, of course. If they're going to kill me off, then they had better be ready for me when I get there. I have the money to throw around, and they may even use it to do a little good for the world. Now, please don't interrupt. This morning was about you, but this afternoon is about me."

Isaac looked down at his notes before continuing. "Over the next four weeks, my condition will deteriorate rapidly. One of the best doctors in the field is managing my pain, but my demise is certain. Rather than wasting away completely, I have decided that I will go exactly when and how I choose. After all, I have the money, so I can do whatever the hell I want. My plan is simple enough. I will be placed into a deep coma and given the strongest painkillers. Then, when I am close to death, I would like to be cremated with $5 million in cash. We will burn together while we both still have currency!"

Isaac had expected a protest but not the tsunami of horror that hit him next. Even Steven, who had only just met him, was pleading for Isaac's life. Susan and John had an expression of disbelief on their faces, and all three of them were on their feet.

"You want us to burn you alive? You have *got* to be kidding,' Susan exclaimed.

John echoed her sentiment, adding, "I won't have any part of it!"

"It's the only way to ensure that I die at the right time," Isaac replied.

This time it was Steven with the question. "What *right time*? You're asking us to break so many laws here — one of which is murder, by the way."

Isaac calmed himself. "I need to ensure that I leave this earth at exactly the same time as my money. Let me remind you all that this is no pro-life debate. I'm dying anyway. There is nothing that can be done. No more experimental therapies to cling to, no god to pray to. I've seen what's coming, and it's not pretty. I just want to choose the moment and method of my death. It only needs to be minutes before I would expire naturally anyway. I am not asking you to murder me. Just drive me to the cliff and let gravity do its work, so to speak."

All present were silent as the weight of the request hung in the air. Isaac allowed it to play out. He could not physically execute this plan alone and wanted his people with him till the end. At some point, each of them formed the beginning of a word on their lips but let it pass.

Finally, Isaac had waited long enough and pointed to their chairs. "Please, sit. I've always made sure that I was in complete charge here. My ego wouldn't settle for anything less. However, in this matter, I will give you two the choice." He gestured to Steven. "You are going to do what you're told — that is, if you want the money."

Susan surrendered. "You're the boss. I have never questioned you before. Why start now?"

Finally, Steven spoke. "I have no choice. The bookies have

already said that they'll kill me if I don't come up with the money by the end of the month. These aren't your every-day track guys. These are mobsters," he chuckled nervously. "I may actually have a shorter life span than you, Mr. McGlynn."

Isaac laughed. "I've already made a tentative deal with their boss. I told him that, if you accepted my proposal, I would pay him half right away if he keeps his men away. If you make sure that my will is incontestable, my death wishes are respected and nobody goes to jail in the process, I will pay the rest at the end of the month. The money left over will go to you."

Steven let out a sigh of complete relief. "Thank you, Mr. McGlynn.

"Call me Isaac. Now I *own* your ass!"

"Just like he owns ours," Susan added.

Isaac was mentally exhausted. Susan — referring to her own fine ass, even if only as a joke — had completely broken his concentration.

"Okay. Time to get out of my office," he said. "Susan, get him a desk and whatever else he needs, and then get back in here as soon as possible. I'm aching everywhere, and you have the best hands in the business. You would never deny a dying man his last wish, would you?"

"*Never,*" she said with a twist of pity.

Deathbed

———◆———

ISAAC'S "STEPS TO DEATH" PLAN had been progressing well. He had addressed it every morning and demanded updates from his team every night. He also had a doctor who was willing to assist for that same million-dollar handshake the lawyer had accepted. Instead of gambling debts, this money promised to lift the noose of a terminal illness for one of the doctor's children. Even for doctors, the best medicine could often be out of reach.

Assisted suicide was legal in their state. However, the methods that Isaac had in mind would never be sanctioned. He needed to provide the doctor with a get-out-of-jail-free card. Isaac instructed Steven to prepare a fallback contract for the doctor, stating that Isaac had formally requested his assistance in his death. Isaac needed to state on paper — and on video — that he had made the decision while mentally competent and under extreme pain, and that the request was made without coercion or manipulation.

If all went according to plan, nobody — outside of John, Susan and Steven —would ever see the contract or know the doctor's identity. The only reason that Steven knew the doctor's name was to write it in the contract should it ever be needed to keep the man out of jail. For his part, the doctor had agreed to administer the almost lethal dose of anesthetic but flatly refused to stay around for what was planned next. It wasn't the death itself that worried him. It was the cold self-brutality of Isaac's plan.

* * *

Three weeks had passed. In that short time, Isaac's body had deteriorated rapidly. He was now confined to his bed, so the resources of his office had to be relocated to his home.

Since the day he had broken the news to his team, he was no longer physically able to call on Susan for any of her special work duties. In a show of pity, she had offered to show him her bare breasts at a moment when the pain had gripped him tightly and refused to let go. The painkillers weren't working, and she had hoped that a distraction would help. However, he thought it better not to whet an appetite he could not satisfy.

He called the team together for a final review of the plans, and they sat around his bed.

"Soon it will be too difficult to give you instructions," he began. "I know you think that I'm a little crazy, but I'm still determined to go through with this. I need to know now if any of you are having second thoughts."

He scanned the room — not for their words but to read the truth on their faces. If there was any doubt hiding behind their eyes, he would see it. This was his superpower in business. John had once called him "a human bullshit detector."

The three heads hung low, but their expressions were resolute. They weren't happy about his plans, but either they respected him enough or the money was too much to turn down. Isaac was quite sure they would do it.

Susan did her own quick scan of the room and spoke for the group. "No, boss. If this is what you want, then we're with you."

"Good. Do you have the money ready?" Isaac asked John, who now had full access to his bank accounts.

"Yes. I have the money for everyone in envelopes, ready to go."

"The money for the coffin?" Isaac snapped.

"Sorry. Yes, it's ready. Packed into the walls of the coffin. It's in the room next door. Five million, just as you requested."

Isaac relaxed slightly. There was still much to do, and he was already exhausted. "Susan, talk to me about the cremation process."

By now, Susan was accustomed to providing daily updates to Isaac and had her notes prepared. "Okay. I've confirmed that they can cremate up to 440 pounds, so there will be no problem getting you and the money into the furnace. By law, they're not allowed to open the casket on arrival, so they should be none the wiser of what's inside. We have a firm booking for next Tuesday, which is when they think the funeral is. I told them that your express wish is to be cremated within one hour of your funeral for religious reasons. They needed a death certificate, which I've already emailed them, thanks to our friend the doctor. Lastly, I took the full-service cremation. Any stupid upsell they had, I took. It was only a few extra thousand dollars, and it seemed to stop them from asking further questions."

"Perfect. Thank you, Susan. This was never part of our deal. I am truly sorry to ask it of you."

"You are a dying man, and this is your wish. Besides, we have a *new* deal." Her last sentence was accented with a smile for his benefit. Underneath, it was clear that she was still sad about the situation.

Isaac returned her smile to the best of his ability and then turned to Steven. "How are we with the paper trail? Will, contracts, deeds, etc. Is it all done? Do all the details and the dates match up?"

Steven had the air of a man whose job was done but not to his satisfaction. "Yes, it is complete. I've compiled copies of everything and given them to John. I just wish that we could have gotten a second pair of legal eyes to be sure."

"Don't worry. We did," Isaac assured him. "John, what did your man have to say?"

John pushed a collection of loose, marked-up papers across the table. "He had a few minor suggestions. Overall, he said that it was a thorough job, given the time frame and the amount of money involved."

"You had someone *else*?" Steven asked. "Why didn't you just use them in the first place?"

Isaac put up a hand to calm him. "Let's just say that we didn't have the same leverage over him that we did with you. Either way, you wanted to have a second pair of eyes. You got them. And it sounds like you've done a good job." Isaac paused for a moment to consider if he might need Steven for anything else, and then turned to John. "John, you can release the money to Steven's bookie and give Steven the envelope with the remaining cash."

Steven's professional ego threatened to protest, but his personal relief steadied his nerve. Isaac knew that he was now gambling debt free, without the threat of physical violence for himself and his family. He had gone from living on death row to becoming a rich man in three weeks. It had been the ultimate get-out-of-jail-free card, and now his wife would never have to know how close they had come to losing everything.

"Thank you, Isaac. You know, it's a shame we didn't meet earlier. I think I would have liked working for you."

John laughed. "Steven, you're only smiling now because you delivered to Isaac what he wanted. If you had made a mistake, it may have been a different story."

The three of them laughed, but the warning to Steven was clear: Don't get too comfortable around Isaac McGlynn or his people. Leave while you're ahead, and don't push your luck.

Steven got up to leave. "Well, anyway, thank you, Isaac. If there are any late changes or anything else you need from me, please let me know." He took three steps toward the door and then paused, searching for words. "Oh, and in all seriousness, I hope your death goes well." He left the room with his final words floating in the air.

Race to the Finish Line

B Y THE TIME THE FIRST beams of sunlight finally broke through the window shades of Isaac McGlynn's bedroom, he had already been awake for six hours. Sleep had come to him like a thief, sliding in through a window, taking a slice of what precious time he had left, and then disappearing without detection.

The sliver of life remaining in his body had much less physical substance to grip. It had mostly given up on his limbs and retreated to what remained of his vital organs. His face resembled old leather, pulled loosely over a plastic Halloween skull. The skin of his arms and legs took the form of cold, rotten meat, and even his own smell disgusted him. Pain itself was the only reminder that his body was still alive.

The worst part of the last week was the excessive amount of time he'd had to think. He was learning that a thought or memory could start small but grow like a cancer in his mind. Pivotal moments from his past were pondered and reconsidered from every possible angle until they became so encompassing that even a self-inflicted blow to the head could not have forced his mind to move on. Had he made the right decisions at the right times throughout his life? Did he owe John or Susan an apology for anything he had done for them, or should he just be happy with the leadership that he provided? No consideration was too small.

The only solution that Isaac had was to redirect his thoughts elsewhere. Deep down, he knew that dying with his money was potentially the most pointless and wasteful thing he would have ever done. Still, he didn't care. It was about taking control of death and not allowing it to take from him what he had spent a lifetime working for.

* * *

Isaac's nurse came into his bedroom with a glass of water and a small cup of pills.

He pushed the pain aside and allowed himself a moment of bravado. "Not today. When death comes for me ..." The pain in his stomach forced him to take a sharp breath, but then he continued. "I want to feel its breath on the back of my neck."

His voice no longer commanded a room. It barely made it past his bed. It simply left his mouth and travelled to her ear like a whisper in the wind.

The nurse, accustomed to difficult patients, tried to refuse him. "Now, you take your medicine, Mr. McGlynn. Nobody is dying today."

"Oh, how wrong you are!" Isaac thought.

He pointed feebly over his shoulder to the bedside drawer. She opened it, and it was full of money. On his insistence, the nurse withdrew a fistful of hundred-dollar notes.

"I don't need anything further from you today," Isaac said into the air. "Please take the money and go."

It had been days since he had been able to maintain eye contact with anyone other than Susan.

The nurse took the money reluctantly. "So, I'll see you tomorrow, yes?"

"No. No Isaac tomorrow."

Their short conversation was starting to tax him now. His rattled breathing became shallower.

His reluctance turned her face to sadness. "I've seen death many times, Mr. McGlynn. He is not ready for you today. Let him wait a few extra days."

"*Good,*" Isaac thought. "*If he is not ready, then I will catch him unaware.*" But all he had the energy to say was, "Go."

The nurse left and Susan entered. She waited until the door had closed and they were alone before approaching Isaac's bed.

Her voice was seductive and sweet. "It's a beautiful morning, Isaac. If I had to leave this world, I would want to remember it like this. Are you ready? Everything is in place."

Isaac was proud of her. Even on his deathbed and with his money already as good as in her account, she was still not questioning his orders.

Exhausted from his conversation with the nurse, all Isaac could say was, "Yes."

Susan kissed him on the cheek, walked back to the door and held it open for the doctor. He passed her without a side glance and went straight to Isaac. He looked like a man who wanted to leave the premises as soon as possible.

He took out a pen light and shined it in Isaac's eyes. "Isaac, I am only going to ask you this once, so please consider your answer. Any waiver and I will not proceed. Do you still intend to end your life today?" He already had the video testimony safely locked away at his practice, so this was just a formality.

"Yes," Isaac replied, stealing himself against his internal quiver. Every throttled breath brought pain and every limb ached.

The doctor let out a sigh, clearly hoping instead for a late reprieve of his duty. "Okay then. I'll get on with it." He turned to Susan. "Can you get John and the casket in here please? I want witnesses, and I'll need him to help me lift Isaac when it's done."

Susan left. The doctor took one last look into Isaac's eyes before performing his duty. He opened his medical bag and removed assorted syringes and bottles.

"Now, as I said to you last week, Mr. McGlynn, I can bring you close to death ... to the edge of the cliff, so to speak. What I can't guarantee is that you won't simply roll over of your own accord — though part of me hopes you will," he said. He looked over his shoulder to make sure they were still alone. "This is an inexact science. All I can say to you is that I will honor our agreement by putting you in a medically induced coma. The sort of coma that nobody ever comes back from. I expect you will stay deep in that state for at least the next few days if you were to live that long. We know that coma patients do not usually feel physical pain. When they finally flick that switch, will you feel it? Probably, but there is no one alive who can answer that question."

The door opened. John and Susan wheeled in a coffin fit for a king — a *big* king. The walls of the box were intricately inlaid with a gold pattern, which seemed to mimic the roots of an eternal tree. They left the coffin on the far side of Isaac's bed and joined the doctor by Isaac's side.

The doctor set about his task, inserting upright syringes into bottles and flicking the tips once. He paused one last time. He had prepared patients for death before but never like this, and never with a suitcase full of cash waiting for him by the door.

Susan took the doctor's hand assertively. "Do it."

John's face was a picture of wild bewilderment. After all the planning, it was clear that John had harbored doubts whether the plan would ever play out. He took an audible breath and was about to say something when Susan cut in.

"*Stop!* Whatever you're about to say, don't. This job is hard enough for everybody already. Don't make it worse."

"Okay," John said, wringing his hands together. "I'll check that everything is okay outside. You continue in here without me." Looking down at Isaac, he added, "So sorry Isaac. I just can't watch this step."

Isaac didn't judge John for his reluctance in that moment. For all his muscle, John had never had the strength of mind of himself or Susan. Isaac still had two willing accomplices to follow the plan to the end.

The doctor took Isaac's arm, and the needle broke skin. Even though Isaac's body was a perfect storm of pain, the needle found space to make itself known, and he welcomed it like an old friend come to take him away.

Isaac felt an internal flood as the toxin entered his system. Susan's pained smile was the last thing he saw as his eyes closed. In that moment, he saw her not as simply desirable or attractive but instead radiating with an aura that he had never noticed before. Unlike him, she was fully alive — not clinging to the edges — and life itself was magnificent.

Susan and the doctor exhaled as the body lying in front of them transformed from a pained existence to a comatose shell. Isaac's heavy breathing stopped abruptly.

The doctor checked for a pulse, and then put his hand over Isaac's mouth as a secondary check. He looked at Susan and, after a few moments, broke the silence. "Well, I must admit that I didn't think he would survive this far, but he has. He's still in there somewhere, holding onto life."

"He's stronger than he looks, which is why I chose him," Susan said. She allowed the doctor a moment to collect himself before adding, "You take his shoulders, and I'll get his legs. Let's carry him to the coffin."

"Should we call John back in to help?" the doctor asked.

"No. I want to do it." Her tone of voice no longer sounded like an international model; instead, it sounded like a small-town, everyday girl.

A Life Up in Smoke

―――・――

THE DARK RECESSES OF ISAAC's mind constructed its own dreamscape for remaining consciousness to reside. It was to become the last known living address of Isaac's soul.

His mind created a river with its waters flowing steadily and unrelenting toward an unknown destination. Isaac smelled the trees and bushes at its banks and tasted the minerals within the water as it splashed against his cheeks. The water was warm enough to not chill his body and cold enough to be refreshing, and something about the combination made him feel safe in its embrace. His mind simply floated like a leaf along its current. He may have floated in that fashion for a flicker of an eyelid or an entire lifetime. He had lost his concept of time but not direction. He knew that he was traveling somewhere and that it was important.

Without warning, the scene in front of him suddenly changed. He dropped violently through rapids and an enormous roar of angry water filled his ears. He couldn't see what was ahead, but he knew, even in this state, that every rapid led to a waterfall and he was not quite ready to face the cliff.

Although a part of him had been present in the water, Isaac did not have his full physical form, so he found the need to pull himself together. Through sheer force of will, Isaac imagined an arm and a torso. Seeing his success, he then imagined a tree fallen across the river ahead, directly before the river mouth. As he approached it, he grabbed its branches with all his might and stopped his descent a foot before the fall. His grip was strong, but the pull of the water was unrelenting. Within minutes, he knew that he would lose the battle if he did not correct the situation. He tried to imagine the rest of his body, but panic gripped him. With diminished focus, he imagined a second arm. Then, with both arms available, he pulled his torso out of the water and spread his weight across the branch.

Isaac took a moment to look around. His vantage point was only slightly above the water, but it gave him enough information to evaluate his situation. Outside the riverbank, there were no treetops or overgrown grass, no rocks or clearings, no world at all outside of the river. He looked upriver, from where he had come, but again only saw the water and an embankment on either side, spanning about 5 feet each way.

He had two options: continue to hold onto the tree and wait or return to the water and let it take him to its destination. For the moment, he held.

* * *

With great care, Susan and the doctor lifted Isaac's limp body into the custom-made coffin. They affixed a portable life-support system for his breathing, which would give him a few hours of air — likely all that he would need — to ensure that Isaac did not suffocate on the way to his preordered death.

"It seems such a waste," the doctor said to Susan as he ran his hand over the lining into which John and Susan had stuffed as much money as they could fit. "All this money going up in smoke. Imagine how many lives could be saved by this money." The doctor's face drifted into thought while he considered what he might be able to do with it. "You know, he's as good as dead already. I couldn't bring him back from that cocktail even if I wanted to. There's no point in all this money perishing as well."

"Don't you touch it!" Susan snapped. "He kept his word, and you got your money. If you knew anything about him, you would know that you don't steal from Isaac McGlynn — even in death." She reached for her purse and pulled out a small handgun. "Besides that, if you touch a single dollar in that casket, I will kill you myself."

The doctor searched her face for a sliver of weakness and found none. He put his hands up slowly. "You're right. I have my money and I've honored my end of the deal. My girl will get her medicine and that's all I should be interested in. I'm truly sorry for your loss. He tried to change the subject by saying, "Do you need a hand wheeling him out to the car?"

Susan took a long look at him and then seemed happy that the threat had passed. "No, it's okay. John and I can do it. You can go. If you see my colleague on the way out, can you please send him in?"

The doctor collected his money and wished her well before leaving her alone in the room with Isaac.

* * *

Susan pushed the lid down, locking the casket and sealing Isaac into his cash-loaded funeral pyre. Earlier, the lock was altered to ensure that no one at the crematorium could open the casket and suddenly find themselves a windfall. Susan had the only key safely stashed away in a safe in her apartment in case of an emergency, and not even John knew that it existed. She was determined that it never be used.

She collected her bag and placed it on top of the coffin so that she could use both hands to push it out to the car. As she pushed it toward the door, Susan didn't break her stride as John joined her in the doorway from the other side.

"Ah, let me get that for you," he said, holding the door wide open. Once the coffin was far enough through, John jogged to the front to help push. "Sorry about before. Something just felt off to me. I said my goodbyes already. As much as I loved him, I just couldn't watch it."

"It's all we've been talking about for the last two months," Susan replied."

"I know, I know. I guess a small part of me just never expected him to go through with it."

"That's because *you* didn't have to find a doctor desperate enough to end someone's life. That discussion wakes you up to the whole situation very quickly. Let's get this done. I am not going to be comfortable until Isaac and his cash are in ashes."

At the mention of Isaac's burial cash, John's face twitched. Susan wasn't sure what it meant, but she silently commended herself for having the new lock installed on the casket.

* * *

A hearse was waiting in the driveway with its rear door open and the driver standing patiently by the side.

John's nervousness was playing out for all to see. "Here's one for you," he said to the driver. "He's still warm too."

This black humor took the driver by surprise, who until that point had the demeanor of a man not used to being spoken to. He smiled a little and said, "Ah, okay. Thanks." He may have had his own jokes about the dead among his friends, but he did not seem comfortable sharing them with customers.

Susan gave the driver an apologetic look, and he nodded. His expression seemed to say, "They all react differently."

Once the casket was secure, the driver, John and Susan each started their thirty-minute drive to the crematorium. Susan welcomed the time alone and prepared herself for what was to come.

John changed the radio station in his car eight times before giving up in frustration and running his hands through his thinning brown hair. He could handle violence; in fact, he enjoyed it. The voluntary death of his old friend was another story.

The moment the driver was out of earshot of the others, he serenaded the comatose Isaac with his own version of Aerosmith's greatest hits. It was not one of his finest vocal moments, but it was good enough for a rich, dead man.

* * *

Isaac clung to his tree as the river of his life rushed past him. In this new world, he was a fragment of his full self with a blind desire to stay alive through creation of his own iron will. Every physical bump in the real world threatened to dislodge his grip in the dream, but he held firm. He didn't know why, but he knew that he would let go when the time was right.

* * *

The crematorium that Susan had selected did not usually create or house the ashes of the super-rich. It had been chosen for its selective blindness to certain protocols as long as the fee was large enough. It marketed itself as "the state's only drive-through crematorium." It was a joke constructed on the fact that a hearse could drive right into the building and out the other side without having to turn.

Susan thought, *"A more fitting motto might have been, 'Let's get this over with!'"* She parked her car and ran inside, keen to ensure that she had a line of sight to the casket wherever possible until its final end.

The owner of the business met her with a sad nod and a low voice, which she was sure had been enhanced for effect. "Hello, Miss Susan. It is lovely to see you again. I only wish it were under better circumstances. I ..."

Susan didn't wait for him to finish. "Is everything ready?" She pointed to the casket and then toward the back of the building where their equipment was housed.

The owner was not used to being rushed. "Why, yes. Everything is just as you requested. We will wheel him around now. Don't you want to wait for the others to come?"

"No. Let's get it done," Susan answered, shaking her head from side to side. "And I don't need any of that 'sorry for your loss' crap!"

"Yes, okay. I understand." The owner may have been hoping to press her for a little more money, but now Susan had pushed the thought completely out of his mind. She was beautiful but not a pushover.

According to Susan's wishes, she and the owner had completed all the paperwork during the previous week to ensure that the cremation could take place without delay. It had been the only condition that had stalled their negotiations due to strict regulations within the industry. She had been tempted to let it go and take care of it on the cremation day but attending to detail was what Susan did. She pushed on, and they found a way.

The owner gestured to his son, who had the same look on his face that many men had when Susan walked into a room.

"Hey, boy!" the owner finally said in frustration and with a little embarrassment.

Afraid that he might look simple in front of Susan, the young man jumped to attention, ran over to the casket and wheeled it into place, saying eagerly, "It's ready!"

His father pushed him aside and regained Susan's attention. "Now, are there any last words you'd like to say?"

"Which button do I press?"

At that moment, John walked in. The owner pointed to a red button with its own safety switch.

Susan had never flinched when given an instruction from Isaac, and she wasn't about to start now. Without hesitation, she reached out and pushed it. As John strolled casually over to her, expecting to be part of some ceremony, she announced, "It's done!"

* * *

In the recesses of Isaac's mind, he knew that his time had come. An all-engulfing fire was burning the world around him from every perceived angle. The two arms he had imagined started to ignite and blister, bringing with it a pain that he had never thought possible. He held onto the tree branch as firmly as he could, ready to jump at the right moment.

Only the bones of his fingers were visible, and his body was almost completely engulfed in a pain that could only be described as absolute. In that moment, he understood everything and remembered who he was and why he was there.

It's wasn't just him burning. His money was burning as well. If he wanted to pass over with it, then it was time to let go. Unfortunately, leaping to your death wasn't as easy as it sounded in his head. His mind was willing, but his limbs were reluctant right up to the moment he left the branch. As he jumped into the abyss, he opened his senses to capture as much as he could.

At that moment, Isaac McGlynn's life went up in smoke.

Heaven: A Nice Place to Visit

———•———

ISAAC'S FIRST MOMENTS IN HEAVEN were the strangest experience of his life. He had physical form again, but he wasn't wearing his body the way he used to. The hair on his head seemed unsure which way to fall and having nothing visual to focus on left him disoriented.

"Welcome, Mr. McGlynn!" said a cheery male voice that was everywhere and nowhere.

The moment the male voice had finished, Isaac heard no sound at all. It made him wonder if he had lost connection to it.

Then the voice continued. "Sorry. Let me make this easier for you. I'll get out of your head for starters."

Right in front of Isaac, a young man materialized. He wasn't anatomically correct, and his right arm was slightly lower than it should have been.

"Sorry," it said, analyzing itself limb by limb and adjusting like a human puzzle. "It's been a while since I have done this, and I'm not sure I'm getting it right."

It moved the arm up to its correct position. The hair

grew a little too long and then became short again, receding against its skull. Finally, its eyes cycled through colors like a jackpot machine.

The body in front of him was naked, so he looked down. There was new skin where the genitals should be. It was like looking at a real-life Ken doll with a plastic mold in place of his manliness.

"Oh! Excuse me. I should get some clothes on," the Ken doll said, bemused but not entirely embarrassed.

Rather than adding clothes as an outer layer, it simply created clothes from skin already present. The clothes were impossible to date by style or fabric. It had simply chosen a standard torso covering and pants.

"We've been very keen to meet you!" it said, trying its best to match the facial expressions to the words but overacting in the process. It had the sort of face that merged every race into one. No feature — ears, eyes, nose or mouth — stole attention from the other but instead held its place in the puzzle. "You see, we know so little about you, and well, you know what they say: A change is as good as a holiday."

Isaac felt around for his arms and legs and was happily surprised to find himself whole again.

"Where am I, and who are you?" he said, a little disgusted at the display of human origami that had just played out in front of him.

"Good questions. Oh, this is going to be fun!" it said, rubbing its new hands together like an excited child. "You could say that you are in heaven, but there are so many other names we could use. I think you called it heaven, so let's go with that. Now, who am I?" The figure paused, putting its finger to its cheek in an exaggerated thinking gesture. "To be honest, I'm not really sure anymore. I do know this: I am here to help you."

"If I am in heaven, then where is God? Where are the angels?"

The figure clapped its hands and looked around excitedly. "I don't know! I have never seen them. But if you say they are here, I'm sure they are."

Isaac looked past the form. "Then who is in charge?" He hated to have his time consumed by fools.

The form got excited again. "Oh, I know *this* one! Is it you? Or maybe me. These questions are hard."

Isaac rubbed his temples. In doing so, he noticed that his hands had burn scars. In the moment, it seemed worth noting, but he had bigger priorities to consider.

"You said that you were here to help me, but you aren't answering any of my questions," Isaac said flatly.

"I'm sorry. Perhaps you are not asking the right questions. Try some other questions." The form looked perplexed. "It's been so long since I have had to use a body or words. I might be getting them wrong. Let me mature a little and perhaps I can be more helpful that way."

The figure winked at Isaac and pushed facial hair out of its cheeks while graying the hair on its head. Isaac guessed that this little parlor trick gave it an extra thirty years of aging. The teenager was gone and was replaced by what looked like a man in his late forties.

Isaac took a moment to collect his thoughts. On Earth, you would say that he took a breath; in this new place, he didn't need air in his lungs. This sudden realization was suffocating.

When Isaac finally collected himself and spoke again, he

was much calmer and had decided to ask small questions before big ones. "Look, fella. I get that I'm probably dead and in some sort of afterlife, so let's start again. Who are you? And who is the 'we' you're referring to?"

The form furrowed its perfect eyebrows. "Who I am is almost irrelevant. You can call me Fella, if you like. I am presenting to you right now as one person to not overwhelm you." It raised its hands to its cheeks and continued. "Behind me are many! I am answering on behalf of all."

"How many, Fella?" Isaac asked, already comfortable with the new name.

"Many, many!" Fella replied, indicating with wild, sweeping arms that it was more than could be counted.

"If there are so many to draw from, then why is it so hard to get a straight answer?"

"You of all people should know, Mr. McGlynn, that getting an answer from one person is easy. Getting an answer from many is difficult."

"Great. Death by committee," Isaac said to himself in frustration. "You said earlier that you were keen to meet me and that you knew so little about me. Do you say that to everyone?"

Fella smiled. "No, Mr. McGlynn. You are new to us. Nobody has been watching you. Nobody has been paying attention, which is rare. You see, that is our job here."

Isaac was unsure if he should feel special or completely unimportant. A small part of him had always felt unseen. Having no mother or father enabled him to make decisions or act without conscience. He had never had to see disappointment in the eyes of a loved one. He'd known no limits.

"So, your job is watching people. What are you looking for?"

"What are we *looking* for? That is a tough question. Let us think about it for a moment," Fella said. After a pause, he continued. "We can't answer that easily. There are many opinions. There is a saying in the world where you come from: 'If a tree falls in a forest and no one is around to hear it, does it make a sound?' Well, you could say that, if a life is not being watched, did they really live? We watch, so they can live." He seemed pleased with himself for having provided a simple summary to a complex issue.

"And yet nobody was watching me. Does it mean that I didn't live?" Isaac asked with a touch of sarcasm.

Fella responded quickly with assurance. "It seems that you did, Mr. McGlynn. It can happen sometimes — a half-life, if you will — although I'm sure that you may not have thought so. However, with no great love in your life and no children, even you might ask yourself if you were really living. We first caught sight of you in the sorrows of Miss Mitchell. Then her witness came back here and asked a few questions. And, just like that, we found a new soul. Happy days!"

"Miss *Mitchell*? I don't know anyone named Mitchell," Isaac said, caught off guard. He was used to knowing everything.

Fella giggled. "That's right. Susan didn't give you her correct last name, did she? Full of surprises, that one. Don't worry, you have a lot to learn but plenty of time to do it."

Isaac scoffed. He'd had Susan's background checked, and it had uncovered a brief stint as a teenage model and a few previous roles as an assistant but nothing unusual. If it were true that she had given him a fake name — and he guessed that Fella didn't or couldn't lie — then she had gone to a lot of trouble to cover her tracks.

Isaac was intrigued but dead. He would have to deal with being dead first.

He rewound the conversation slightly in his head. "You mentioned that you first saw me in the sorrows of Susan and something about her witness. What does all that mean?"

"Until that point, you had been adrift in a human ocean, and no one other than the people in your boat were aware that you were even missing. You did not have validation."

Isaac took offense to these words. "I was a rich and powerful man! I had millions of dollars' worth of validation!"

Fella's face turned sad. "Money does not enrich a soul. Your memories are the only currency here — good ones, bad ones. It doesn't really matter. They should be the only things that you bring with you. Please give yourself time to absorb that fact and learn everything you will need to know here. I promise that I will answer every question you ask of me to the best of my ability. The more you know now, the less you will understand later. We have some things to do first, which may help you understand."

"Okay. So, what happens now? Where do I go from here?"

"Well, as they say, heaven is a great place to visit, but you wouldn't want to live here," Fella said with a small chuckle. "When you finally do stay with us, it will be because you have nothing left to offer the living, and they have nothing left to offer you. Before we send you back, Mr. McGlynn, let me ask you this: How well do you know yourself? How well do you know your moments? I'm talking about those tipping-point moments when your life changed. Have you ever heard the saying, 'My life flashed before my eyes'? Well, don't blink, Mr. McGlynn, or you might miss it!"

In that instant, Isaac's new world disappeared, and he plunged into darkness.

Born from Death

————•————

ISAAC'S NEW SETTING WAS so black that he wasn't sure if his eyelids were open or shut.

The sound of a hollow ignition hit his senses like the strike of a steel match on flint in an echo chamber. A bouncing speck of light burst into a miniature life form in front of him. It hovered in the air like a firefly crossed with a sparkler — never quite stationary or moving far from its position. The initial sound evolved into a quavering hiss, which modulated with the movement of the light.

To Isaac's surprise, he found himself counting the seconds while he watched in fascination. It was his own way of imposing a little control in a world that defied existing logic. After eighteen seconds, the behavior of the bouncing speck of light changed, and it started to flash. Sometimes bright and sometimes soft, its rhythm was steady. He couldn't tell if it was getting closer or simply brighter in his vision.

On its next pulse, the light burned brightly and hissed loudly, reaching out and licking Isaac's essence. Even after the light receded, he still felt its love like the aftermath of an incredible kiss. It felt like life itself had just touched him. The sound in his ears had been loud but not physically uncomfortable. Its warmth reassured Isaac that he should not be afraid of what was to come as it would be delivered in love.

The light blinked twice more at a much lower intensity before approaching again. This time, rather than reach out to him, it surged forward and engulfed him completely. The setting had gone from pure black to pure light in an instant. It was compressing him from all sides, and he was being pushed through it like toothpaste in a tube. When Isaac finally made it to the other end of the light, there was a final, mortal squeeze and he landed in a new place.

He saw familiar colors, felt the cool air on his limbs and sensed the familiar anchor of gravity. He was back on Earth! In the first moment, he did not move. It was like sitting in a picture frame. Then, as if someone had lifted their hand from a turntable, it exploded into movement.

Isaac found himself in the passenger seat of a 1970s sedan. Next to him was a young, heavily pregnant girl. She had his color hair and his face shape. Although he had never seen a photograph of his mother, Isaac was absolutely sure that it was her.

"She cannot see or hear you," Fella whispered in his ears. "We want to help you fill in some gaps."

Isaac could not take his eyes off the woman. The car was a small hatchback, so he had to push himself back into his seat to take her all in. As he moved against the leather, it made no sound. Friction was for the living.

The girl—his mother—was crying. Her flowing tears held hands in solidarity as they entered the world two by two. She held the steering wheel in her left hand and her swollen belly in her right. The only time she removed her right hand was to navigate a particularly difficult corner or grab a tissue.

Every few minutes, her sobbing was punctuated by a moan of pain, only to be reduced to the sorrow of the moment afterwards. Misery and pain kept each other company.

Without thinking, Isaac whispered, "Where is my father?"

"That is not part of this story, Mr. McGlynn. Perhaps another time," Fella replied.

Isaac reached out in an attempt to touch her, but his touch stopped a few inches short, as if repelled by the opposing force of a magnet.

Fella's voice was in his ears again. "Sorry, Mr. McGlynn. As they say, you can look but you can't touch."

"I want to touch her ... just once."

"You have been touching her skin your whole life, for it is your own. There are no takeaways in these stories. You don't get to touch, feel or taste anything new. You only get a vision of the past."

Isaac retracted his hand and watched more. Having never met his mother or ever seeing a photo of her, it was an odd feeling. He felt sorry for this young, desperate woman, but she was still a stranger to him. It was not love at first sight.

At that moment, Isaac's teenage mother reached through his lap. This time he felt no repelling magnetic force. She simply plunged her hand through him to her handbag on the passenger seat. Isaac did not feel the warmth of his mother's touch. He felt nothing. She withdrew a small plastic packet of tissues and brought them across to her own lap.

She flicked the tissues over and over in her hand, trying to use her fingertips to find the opening in the plastic before fumbling the packet from her grasp altogether. It slid from her lap and fell to the floor of the car, causing her to momentarily take her eyes off the road. As she reached under the dashboard and found the packet again, she accidentally nudged the steering wheel to the right and veered the car into the right-hand lane.

Isaac instinctively reached for the steering wheel to try and correct it, but his hand went through it like passing through water. He adjusted and readjusted his approach but couldn't exert any pressure against it. He yelled in pure frustration.

Fella interrupted. "You cannot change what is about to happen here for it has already happened."

The tires of a heavy, old truck wailed as the driver slammed on the brakes and blasted his horn. The young woman beside him screamed and instinctively wrenched the wheel in the opposite direction of the noise, forcing her into the path of oncoming traffic. She was still midscream when the collision happened.

The truck, much smaller than the one to her right but still large enough to matter, consumed the woman's car like a shark eating a fish head on. The two vehicles merged into one tangled, spinning mess as they pirouetted across the highway, violently inviting other vehicles into their collision. The original truck to the right, which had blown its horn, made contact, although its driver, having been alerted to the impending danger, had swerved to avoid the worst of it.

Isaac, who was not tied physically to this world, simply removed his consciousness from the inside of the car. He took a moment to let what just happened sink in. He had been given less than two minutes with his mother alive, and now she was likely gone. People were starting to run in their direction, waving down traffic and yelling for help.

Isaac willed himself back into the vehicle and saw her instantly. The tears had stopped, and there was blood in their place. His mother blinked slowly, staring straight ahead, not even stopping when the blood dripped into her eye. She was gasping for air.

There was screaming outside the car. Inside, she was silent apart from the sharp gasps of air, which were getting weaker at every turn. Isaac stayed with her, watching and witnessing her final fight for life.

Isaac had been told nothing about his birth or his biological mother other than the lies that had been designed to hurt him as a child. This scene had not been the birth he imagined in any of his dreams.

"I don't understand. If she dies now, how am I born?" he asked Fella.

"Be witness."

The horrible sound of his mother's rasping breaths filled Isaac's ears. She continued to blink through the shock, but this time something was taking her gaze. She looked at the wreckage before her eyes rested on Isaac.

Surprised to be seen, he studied her face in horror. The agony of the situation was leaving her expression. Instead, mild surprise and confusion spread across her face.

Isaac reached for his mother's face, but the magnetic force stopped him once again. He screamed and then took a moment to let his tears flow unencumbered before regaining his composure.

"Did she just see me, Fella?"

"In a way she did, but it is complicated. The Many Many gave her that vision for what was about to come next."

"What is the Many Many?"

"The fabric of souls that, when combined, enable all existence."

Isaac's teenage mother blinked slowly again. This time, it seemed to be more voluntary. Her mouth did not form the fullness of a smile, but the expression tainted the corner of her lips just the same. She closed her eyes, exhaled and lost consciousness.

Isaac panicked. "What just happened? Is she dead?" he asked, fighting the magnetic force with all his might but still failing to make contact.

Fella's voice was pure sadness. "She knew that there was not enough life left in her for both of you, Isaac. She surrendered her life early and, in turn, we granted you one hour of life within her body. If you were not in the hands of the living by then, you would never have lived at all." After a short pause, Fella asked, "Would you like to see your birth, Mr. McGlynn?"

As Isaac heard these words, sunlight poured into the wreckage. People opened the doors and reached in to free the young woman's body.

"No. I don't want to see her like this anymore. I don't want to remember her face in blood."

The light of the world around him suddenly extinguished like an old tube television being turned off. Isaac was back in darkness with the dancing sparkle of light in front of him.

"What now, Fella?" Isaac asked, defeated.

"Now we continue with the real story of your life."

Alone Together

B ACK IN THE VACUUM OF darkness, the dancing firefly of
light provided Isaac with his only visible distraction. He
sensed that it was sending him a message, that it was life
itself and that it was all that mattered. Isaac looked for a pattern in the light's dance but found nothing, which was part
of the reason he found it so fascinating.

"After all," he thought, "why should life be predictable
now? It has never been so in the past."

The light burned brighter and approached him again.
Once more, he felt the beautiful warmth of reality before
it retreated. It teased him once more but finally, on its third
approach, it engulfed him.

Isaac's new surroundings were a stark contrast to his previous vision. The sun barely peeked through the dirty win-
dows of the car, and the stale scent of dirty clothes was gone.
He was surrounded by an inside world of fluorescent lighting
and the stench of hospital-grade disinfectant.

The smell of the place was more than just disinfectant.
Fear was in the air. Isaac knew instantly where he was, and it
was not a place he had ever wanted to see again. It was part
of the reason that he had bought the land and demolished

the building the moment he built enough personal wealth to comfortably do so.

By the time Isaac held the title to St. David's Orphanage, it had been shut down for seven years after being shaken by numerous allegations of impropriety. Some of the children were seen in public, showcasing extensive bruising and worrisome mental health behavior. It had been the final straw for the local community, which had demanded its immediate closure. Other cases had involved sexual abuse, child isolation and international sales of children.

Isaac went straight on the offensive. "Fella, why are we here? I don't want to see anything that happened here."

"But you must, Mr. McGlynn. Before you can witness others, you need to observe your own life. You must understand who you were before you can judge others for who they are. Do not fear. There is nothing to be gained by experiencing pain twice. You will not have to witness the two encounters you fear the most."

Isaac's soul twisted in on itself. He knew that there were two episodes from within the walls of that orphanage that had forever damaged him. He had spent his life hoping that these two events had merely been broken fragments of horrific dreams masquerading as real memories. That's what he and some of the other children preferred to tell themselves, even though they knew they were wrong.

This time, instead of presenting him immediately with a completed world, this world was being built around him. Firstly, he was shown the surroundings to acclimatize. Then, people were superimposed over the top. They appeared around him as if a painter were frantically waving his brush across a canvas from left to right. As soon as each individual appeared, they sprang into life of their own accord, some even starting conversations with others before the next one had been painted completely. It took only seconds for the world to complete itself.

A small child with dark, curly hair was the last character rendered. He looked like any other child on the surface until Isaac noticed his eyes. Isaac had never seen a single photo of himself as a child, but he had spent a lifetime searching those eyes for answers that never came. He knelt down and tried to look deeply into his smaller self, but it was not a smooth process. The scene jumped and stalled like video buffering over a poor internet connection.

"What's wrong here?"

"It's always hard to calibrate the first time a soul sees itself. It will pass very soon," Fella replied.

As Fella predicted, within a few moments the stuttering had passed, and Isaac was back to looking at himself. He studied the face in wonder and, although it still held a little boyhood charm, it was clear that the child's innocence had vanished.

Isaac Junior looked about four or five years old. His large, almond eyes stole glimpses of the world as his curly locks swept across his field of vision. He wore a green t-shirt, which barely made its way around his small torso, and a pair of brown corduroy pants, which had frayed at every opportunity.

The child looked about the room sheepishly, tightly clutching a small bear like a drowning man clinging to a life vest.

After a few moments of introspection, Isaac allowed himself a moment to look around the room. He didn't specifically remember it, but it wasn't completely foreign to him either. He did not remember the room itself but rather the way it made him feel — cold, alone and unloved.

As the other children in the room went about their business, one of the doors to the room opened. Three men, wearing black priest robes, entered. They smiled at the children, but one — an evil-looking one — smiled differently than the others. It was the sort of thing that an adult might miss but a young child would see. This one man stood in the middle of the other two. Without any doubt, he held the power in the group.

Isaac noticed him right away, but then he knew what to look for. His panic rose the moment he saw the evil man. He recognized his face from the crisis point of every bad dream he had ever had. Although he had buried the memory of it many years ago, that face with its acid smile had caused night sweats well into his adult life.

When Isaac spoke, his voice was that of a child. "Why are we here, Fella? I want to leave this place right now!"

"Mr. McGlynn, we have no desire to dig up old pain. Your main witness in this day is not this man but what's to come next. Allow his shadow to pass, and the sun will rise again."

Isaac felt a small touch of the warmth from the dancing light, which brought him back to his senses.

"Just watch, Mr. McGlynn."

He looked down at his younger self again. Isaac Junior had silently pushed himself into the shadows of the corner. The evil man's conversation with the two other men never faltered, and they hung on his every word. However, the man's eyes told a different story as he searched the room for prey. He was crossing it like a man trying to decide which piglet to slaughter for a feast, almost licking his lips in sinister delight.

As the evil man passed through the children, he allowed his fingers to linger and drag across the tops of their small heads. Some smiled, basking in his attention, while others shivered in fear. He scanned the room and made eye contact with Isaac Junior before registering an internal thought and continuing. Isaac Junior cowered further into himself.

A young girl had gone to even greater lengths to hide. She had positioned herself behind an exposed beam in a wall and was staring blankly into a golden book. The only thing visible to the room was her brown, wiry hair and her book. Although it was a good prop, it would have been better if she'd had time to hold it up the right way instead of upside down.

The three men crossed the room and left through an alternate door, the evil one having made his silent selection for later. The others, it seemed, were completely unaware that their social room had been momentarily turned into a holding pen.

Finally, the door closed like the door of a jail cell, and the immediate danger was over. Isaac Junior was perspiring in a way that a child never should. He detached himself from the wall and allowed himself to become a member of the room again.

The young girl jumped to her feet, snatching a glimpse of Isaac Junior before exchanging books and going to hide elsewhere.

* * *

"Look at him!" one of the larger orphanage boys said, pointing in Isaac Junior's direction. "He thinks that he's Brother Anthony's favorite." This boy hadn't hidden but instead tried to garner the attention of the evil man. Perhaps the attention, no matter how painful, made him feel like the favored pet of a bad master.

Isaac Junior cowered, not fully understanding the implications of what was being said and not liking the attention. The bully took two steps forward and slapped him across the face. Isaac Junior's crying didn't start immediately. First there was a sense of shock, and then the tears came in a wave.

The bully laughed and raised his hand to do it again. It was the same laugh that the evil man who had just left them made whenever the children cried. This boy was mimicking the older man in his torment and passing down the misery.

Another child in the room decided that one tormentor was enough. Isaac Junior and the young girl with the book watched as this dark-haired, pink-faced child quietly got to his feet and crept forward while everybody else was looking at the bully and his target.

The new child stalked five steps toward the laughing bully. In his tiny hands, the new child held a yellow metal toy truck. As the bully, now giddy with power, raised his hand to land a second blow on Isaac Junior, the new boy swung his truck at the back of the bully's head with all his might.

A dull thud was heard as metal hit skull, followed by a short rattle of wheels. The blow did not render the bully unconscious but did enough. It attacked his balance first, the pain hit him and then he screamed. The bully fell to the ground, clutching the back of his head and blinking hard to keep himself awake. Droplets of blood rolled and fell from his head to the floor like fat rain before a lightning storm.

The bully's first henchman, who stood to his left, stared at this new child in disbelief. This henchman was another larger boy with white hair. His eyes didn't look capable of showing any joy, even if he'd had the good fortune to experience it in that place. He was unsure how to react with his leader on the floor and unaccustomed to having to think for himself.

Before the first henchman had a chance to react, the new child started a backswing, but it did not have the same devastating success as the first blow. The first henchman received the reduced impact to the side of his face. While it wasn't enough to knock him off balance, the shock did enough damage, and he fell to the ground in tears.

Isaac did not remember this scene of his life. He looked at his smaller self and saw that he had the exact same look of shock.

The bully scampered to his feet, but his first henchman had already fled. The boy with the truck, Isaac Junior and the second henchman remained. The boy with the truck raised his arm once again to strike the second henchman, but the boy did not wait around to be hit. He yelped and bolted from the room before the truck arc found its third victim.

The boy with the truck turned his attention to Isaac Junior, who had raised his hands to his head in fear. The boy's facial expression may have been difficult for an adult to read, but Isaac Junior understood it. The expression reassured Isaac Junior that the boy would not swing the weapon in his direction.

Isaac Junior lowered his hands and looked blankly at him for a moment before his tiny face shifted. It was a small

change, but Isaac recognized it right away. For the first time
in his small life, he felt protected and safe. In that moment,
his face had been set like soft clay that had been finally hard-
ened in a furnace. This face had been with him for as long as
he could remember.

The boy sat next to Isaac Junior. Neither said a word, but
each sized up the other's worldly possessions: one slightly
dented toy truck and one small, grubby teddy bear. The boy
held out the truck without a word, and Isaac Junior took it.
He allowed himself a moment to turn it over in his hands and
marvel at its effectiveness before finally allowing his bear to
be exchanged.

They examined each other's toys for a few moments before
a crash on the other side of the room reminded them that
they were not alone. Isaac Junior handed back the truck
quickly and seemed relieved to have his new friend armed
again. From that point on, they never left each other's side.

* * *

Isaac felt a sense of closure as he watched the two boys. "So,
this is how I met John? I had forgotten all of this," he said,
ensuring that the door through which the evil man had gone
was still closed. "I suppose that some of it I had forgotten on
purpose."

"You never really forgot though. Did you, Mr. McGlynn?"
Fella reminded him. "You came here often in your
nightmares."

"I guess so." He was not used to having someone in his
thoughts and was not enjoying the experience. "Are we done
here? I have had enough of this place."

"Always so quick to leave the living, Mr. McGlynn. I wonder why?" Fella said these words like a man who only asks questions he already knows the answers to. "Are you so sure that this is all you needed to see here? Sometimes the devil is in the details."

Isaac took another long, sweeping look around the room, trying to take in as much of it as possible. He completed one full rotation in frustration, and then something hit him like an electrical charge to his soul.

"Oh, my god!" Isaac gasped, pointing his spiritual hand to a corner of the room. "The girl with the book!"

Immediately, Isaac's world went black once again.

Souls for Sale

———•———

IT FELT LIKE ISAAC'S HEAD was dunked underwater halfway through taking a deep breath. One word was all he needed to say, but he couldn't. He had been completely shocked by what he had just witnessed and wasn't sure if what he had seen was real.

Back in the vacuum of pure, black space with the dancing sparkle of light at play in front of him, he was unable to talk. His mind screamed her name, but it gave him no satisfaction or nourishment. He needed to hear himself say it, to breathe through the word and feel its timbre in his throat.

"Susan?"

Could it be possible that she had been at the orphanage with him and he didn't know it? Surely not. It was probably his mind playing tricks with familiar faces, but those eyes … he knew those eyes. He knew them in a way that one might know a work of art intimately without ever understanding its truth.

The dancing sparkle of light played in front of him once again but this time without its normal vibrancy. It almost extinguished itself before springing back to life stronger and more assured than before. When it approached him at first, its warmth did not touch him with the depth of the past. On the second approach, it touched him lightly like the sun battling a cool breeze on a winter's day.

When the light finally engulfed him on its third pass, the new scene took much longer to present itself for inspection than the last episode. Isaac was back at the orphanage — he could tell that immediately — but life was colder this time. He wasn't sure if it was the overcast weather or the failed system that brought him there. Regardless, he felt it in his essence. It instantly killed the buzz that he had been harboring since leaving his last visit.

"Fella," he said with pain in his soul, "why are we back here? What do I have to gain by digging up the horrors of this place?"

"Your soul, of course. Believe me, Mr. McGlynn, you will need it for what's to come," Fella replied curtly. "But don't worry. You are safe with me. We are simply here to witness."

"Wait, please! Can we stop for a moment? I need time to collect my thoughts. This is too much to take in all at once. I have questions first."

While the world around him had taken minutes to build, its activity stopped in an instant as if someone had clicked pause on a wrap-around cinema screen. Each character was frozen in motion, waiting for release.

Fella materialized, looking slightly different this time. It was the same man-creature but with a slight twist: an ethnicity that Isaac had never seen before. It was like looking at a man crafted from a new or forgotten cut, with a thin-lipped mouth, circular brown eyes and the cheekbones of a Neanderthal.

Fella smiled but seemed to sense Isaac's uneasiness about his appearance. "Sorry. I should have paid more attention to my form last time. I completely forgot how I put myself together. I can pause for some questions but not for long. Time will slow but not stop for us, Mr. McGlynn. Even in a rewind, we don't have that sort of power."

"What is a rewind, Fella?"

"A rewind is the process of looking back on the core elements of a life, Isaac."

Isaac thought fast to make the most of the opportunity. "Why are we seeing these visions? What am I supposed to make of them?"

"These are important moments in your life. You could say tipping-point moments, when little situations make a substantial difference. A life is made up of these moments. Put them all together, and you paint the spine of a single lifetime. You may need to improvise a little to fill in the blanks and add some color to a personality, but fundamentally you see the person. A soul must first observe itself before it can observe others."

Isaac remembered that he was under a time pressure, but he allowed himself a moment to think. He looked around the room before catching the sight of his own hands. They still bore those burn scars, which he had never had while he was alive.

"Why are my hands scarred like this?"

Fella seemed greatly confused. "We thought that's what you wanted," he answered with complete sincerity. "After all, you did that to yourself. If I recall correctly, you traded your life for those burn scars."

"No," Isaac replied in anger. "I was dying, for God's sake. I had myself cremated to stop the pain."

"Is that really true, Mr. McGlynn? Or did you try to steal from death before he stole from you? There is no point in lying to yourself here. Pride is only for the living. We are running out of time now, but you will be able to ask more questions later. Don't you want to ask me the question that was burning in you only moments ago? Don't you want to hear yourself say her name?"

"Yes. Was that Susan at the orphanage? The young girl?"

"Yes," Fella replied before vanishing again.

"How could I not have known? I am supposed to be the guy who knows everything," Isaac said to himself.

"Maybe you don't know as much as you think you do," Fella whispered in Isaac's ears.

"Maybe," Isaac said reluctantly before the world around him sprang to life once again. He took it all in. He knew there was a story to be told somewhere but couldn't find the thread.

* * *

After a minute, Isaac found himself in a crowd. Isaac Junior was slightly larger now, perhaps another two years older but still a child. He was sitting on a large, brown sofa in the orphanage. As far back as he could remember, this sofa never had a single cushion, but it still provided a bench seat at a bare minimum. To all the children, it had become the position of power within their junior hierarchy. Even the bullies from his last rewind did not dare approach this particular sofa now.

* * *

Isaac's persecution at the hands of these bullies had not completely stopped. They had challenged him once more, three days after their last altercation when John had hurt them. This time, they had punched Isaac in the face during one of the rare occasions that he had been walking alone.

John had wanted to immediately retaliate on Isaac's behalf, but Isaac had held him back. He guessed, rightfully, that the bullies would have been expecting John to come and would have been ready for him. Instead, Isaac had waited until they were asleep, and then had gotten John to attack one of the henchmen as he slept. On the second night, John had attacked the other bully. On the third night, on Isaac's command, John had done nothing. Isaac had waited three more days, allowing anxiety to settle from the main threat before setting John free once more. It had been a master stroke. The three boys had never touched Isaac or John again.

With his internal anger ignited and a human weapon at his disposal, Isaac had channeled everything into owning his new life.

* * *

Back on the big, brown sofa, the two boys sat like a king and his general surveying their empire. The door swung open, and the evil priestly brother entered the room with a stranger by his side. Isaac recognized the stranger right away, even though he did not know his name and never saw him again after this moment. The stranger had been granted a revered place within Isaac's long-term memory — not for his actions but for what he was about to signify to the child. He was the only child adopter whom Isaac would ever remember.

The stranger's gray pinstriped suit stood out from the black robes of the devil, like the sun peeking through the clouds on a rainy day. Isaac knew the cut of the suit because, while alive, he had twice requested his tailors to replicate it after seeing a similar cut in a magazine.

The rich stranger's smile was not like that of the devil who accompanied him. His smile rang truer and more golden. Although others had come to the orphanage over the years looking to adopt, something about this man promised not only a life outside of the orphanage but potentially a good one.

While other children had scurried at the sight of the devil, Isaac Junior had thrown caution to the wind and straightened to his full height. He even suggested that John do the same. Together, they smiled in the stranger's direction, waiting to be noticed.

The rich stranger, walking through the room, searched every child's face thoroughly, looking for an unknown quality that was not immediately obvious. Finally, his attention landed on Isaac Junior and John Junior, and their spirits soared. Seeing this, the devil leaned forward and whispered something into the rich man's ear, who nodded and allowed his eyes to wander once again.

Isaac Junior swiveled in his seat to face John Junior and then turned back toward the two men, clearly confused. "What did he say? Why not me? What did I do wrong?"

The devil caught a glimpse of the distress on Isaac Junior's face and smiled. Isaac Junior would not be leaving with the rich stranger. The devil was not ready to let him go.

The rich man in the gray suit selected a child — an innocent angel with sandy blond hair, freckles and tiny hands. They were introduced to each other and both left the room, hand in hand, neither of them to be seen again. Isaac Junior hated them both.

Isaac knew exactly what was going through his tiny mind. The stranger, with all his money, had the power to choose a life over misery for any of them. His money had allowed him to live an ample life while theirs was bleak. His money was a power that Isaac would spend his life trying to attain, with the plan to come back and save whomever was left.

* * *

When the two men left, every child in the room relaxed. Susan Junior, who had been hiding, stuck out her head from behind a bookshelf to take a quick peak. She had obviously decided that continuing to hide from the world was better than being rejected by it. She stole one quick glance at Isaac Junior before pulling herself back into her cave.

"I remember that stranger," Isaac said to Fella, "but not like this. I remember him and his fancy suit being the reason for the punishment and humiliation that was to come for me later that evening." Isaac pointed to his tiny self and continued. "I remember that robed fucking devil goading me as he flogged me. I remember words like, 'You seriously think he would *want* you? Your own *mother* didn't want you! You are worthless other than to give me pleasure, should I wish to take it from you.' I remember that stranger being the real reason I finally did what I did back then, Fella."

At that point, Isaac realized that he could still cry — if not with real tears, then at least with the sentiment of overwhelming emotion — but he hadn't finished talking.

"You say that you don't want to dig up old horrors, Fella, but that's all you do! I wonder … will you show what happens next, or is that too upsetting for your sensitive eyes? Will you show what I did? Will I get the *pleasure* of seeing the devil die with my own eyes for a second time?" Isaac screamed.

"Is that what you want, Mr. McGlynn?" Fella replied, remaining calm. "I don't think you realize that *you* are telling the story here, not me. After all, it is your story to tell. If you decide that particular part of your story needs to be told, then it will be. We may need to fast forward through some of your adult life."

Isaac thought for a moment while the physical world around him was in suspended animation. His adult life had been full of successes, some of them honestly earned, while others had been taken by force. And, while his adult life had been one of luxury, the early pages of his book had been written in pain and suffering. When you start off your life so far behind the mark, everything else is just catch up, no matter how far in front you get.

"I need to see it again for closure," Isaac admitted, "or it will continue to play in my head like a song you hate but can't stop singing." He took a few breaths to calm himself down for what was to come.

"Okay, but before we leave here, are you sure that you have learned everything this place has to teach you?"

Isaac looked around wildly. "What am I missing?"

"Come with me," Fella said, leading them through the same door the two men and the child had gone through. They entered a small office that Isaac knew only too well. "I think it's important to see a little more of the man you would model your life on."

* * *

In the office, the two men were seated at opposite sides of a brown wooden desk with the robed brother at the business end.

"What is your name, child?" he asked through a thinned smile, the kind that could cut through skin.

The young boy gulped, unused to the attention. "Eric," he replied, stealing glances at both men before finding the focal safety of the floor in front of him.

"Ah, Eric. Yes, I remember now," the robed devil replied as he retrieved a manila folder from the drawer to his right. The devil turned away from the boy and addressed the man directly. "It says here that he was brought in only a few months ago. No living family. Ward of the state. Or, in other words, he belongs to me. And, as we discussed earlier, he could belong to you also for the right fee, of course. I simply burn this paper file, falsify a document and the child disappears."

Isaac was in shock. Coming into this room hand in hand with an adult from the outside world had always seemed like the gateway to a new life. He wasn't exactly sure what he was witnessing: unsanctioned adoption, child slavery or perhaps something even worse?

"Mr. McGlynn, you have been allowed to witness this exchange even though this event was not in your story," Fella explained. "The Many Many felt that it was necessary in order to tell your story more completely."

Isaac continued to watch. The rich man could not take his eyes off the child. He ran his hand down Eric's back and let it rest on his hip.

When the rich man finally spoke, his voice was much deeper than Isaac had expected. "And you say that nobody has touched this child?"

"I give you my word," the robed devil replied. "I alone

would know. As I said earlier, I own these children. Do we have a deal?"

"If you burn that file in front of me, we do," the rich man replied, producing a large bundle of hundred-dollar notes from his jacket pocket.

Isaac guessed that it probably added up to about $10,000. He had paid for all sorts of things in that manner himself. "My god," he said to Fella. "Is that small bundle of money the cost of a life?"

Fella replied with an anger that Isaac had not yet experienced. "*No!* No soul *ever* owns another. All souls are equal. The *living* abuse each other while they are still alive. Sadly, sometimes their hate carries across and they try to abuse each other here, but let's not discuss that now. Do you want to know more about the fate that awaits this poor child, Isaac? After all, you wanted so desperately to be him. Or perhaps the rich man himself? Do you want to know what became of him after he had wrung the essence out of the boy? Is that still the man you want to be?"

"No. I don't want to know," Isaac pleaded. "Can we leave this place now? Please?"

Fella hadn't finished with him yet, and his anger was rising. "Did you know, Mr. McGlynn, that it took four weeks of pure torment at the hands of that monster for this beautiful soul to close his eyes to the real world forever? Four weeks of abuse, molestation and rape before his little body finally gave over. That's longer than you were prepared to suffer your cancer."

"Why are you telling me all this? I didn't do it!" Isaac screamed. "I'm a victim too, remember? Why aren't you screaming for what happened to *me*?"

Fella tempered his response this time. "Because, for this child, there is not a single living person outside of that man who knew or cared that he was dead. What's left of his buried young body still rots on the grounds of the man's property. I want you to reconsider everything you held dear. Your career, your money, your power. You were so determined to be that rich man, who is standing in front of you now. You broke rules and people to do it. Perhaps you may think that, in some small way, you succeeded in your quest. Now that you know the type of person he really is, do you still need all that money and power? And, if not, who are you without it?"

"I don't know who I am."

"Good. That's important, but ..."

Isaac cut him off. "I know one thing for sure though, Fella. Whatever it costs me, I want to see that man die one more time," he said, pointing to the devil in the black robe.

His world went black once again.

Trading a Death
for a Life

WHEN THE DANCING BALL OF light presented itself this
time, it did not project the vibrancy it had on previous occasions. It resembled a timidly burning wick rather
than a vibrating ball of energy. Even if Fella had not already
told Isaac that his rewind time was running out, he could
have guessed it.

Isaac's soul was angry by what he had just seen, but he had
no way of expressing it. Instead, he felt his anger dead in the
heart of his essence. He wasn't even sure if seeing what was
about to come would be any easier as a spectator than it was
as a participant.

The burning wick of light, when it came, engulfed him in
a slow, painless burn. It found extremities that Isaac didn't
know he had and worked its way to his center. He was reborn
out of the ashes like a phoenix into his new rewind world,
back in the same office he had been in earlier.

Isaac took a moment to look at the clock on the wall in the
orphanage office and noticed a detail that he had never seen

as a child: the picture of a tiny crucifix with the slogan "God Is Watching" written just above the number six.

* * *

Eric, who had been purchased eight hours before, was now unsafely residing in his new owner's residence. He had been smuggled into his new mansion home and broken within 15 minutes. The most that he would ever see of this home was a 13 x 20-foot soundproof room, which his new "Daddy" had previously installed under the guise of a music recording studio. The child lay sobbing and bleeding in a corner of the room. Isaac knew all of this without seeing it or being told.

* * *

Fella interrupted his thoughts and said, "Mr. McGlynn, you are tapping into the knowledge of the world. That child's fate is not what we are here for. You are effectively eavesdropping on someone else's life, and you must stop right away or risk losing yourself in the process. Keep your focus on what you can see for yourself, not what has been seen by others. Eric's misery is his own, and he has made peace with it since."

"How do you know that, Fella?" Isaac asked with sincerity, trying to understand as much of his new world as he could.

"I know because he is now part of the Many Many. I question, and I know, because he knew," Fella replied. "Please take my caution that he is not part of your story. You need to concentrate on what will happen in this very room. Don't waste this opportunity."

* * *

Isaac unfocused himself from Fella and instead decided to study his surroundings. If his previous rewinds were anything to go by, he would not have a lot of time till the action took place, so he should not let any detail escape his attention. He was also seeing a pattern where the main story of the rewind was often in the place where he least expected it to be.

Fella sensed the change. "Good. Take it all in, Mr. McGlynn. You will find that your ability to see and remember will increase. You'll need these skills when you observe others."

Isaac saw the same room as in the previous rewind. However, this time it was empty. Its centerpiece — the same brown wooden desk — had a director's chair on one side and two metal collapsible chairs on the other. The design seemed to suggest command and comfort for the host and mild discomfort for any guests.

Two items were exactly where Isaac knew they would be. Firstly, the faded brown leather strap — the weapon of choice for the robed devil — was on the right edge of the desk. Its handle was within easy reach of the director's chair while the majority of its length lay slightly hidden under paper trays.

The other item Isaac recognized right away was a stone plaque, which the orphanage had been given by the city mayor on its opening. It was resting on a pine bookshelf to the right of the director's chair, next to the desk. The plaque was fashioned from an exotic, heavy stone mined from the same town as the orphanage and had become the town's main source of income. Isaac, with all his worldly knowledge, did not know what precise mineral it was. He did know, however, that even a soft blow from it had enough weight to break a child's fingers. He looked down at his right hand and was reminded of the odd angle the knuckle of his fourth finger had.

* * *

The door of the orphanage office swung open, and the black-robed devil drifted in with Isaac Junior in his clutches. The devil's feet hardly touched the ground, but Isaac Junior's never left it. His feet left two trails of rubber as he was dragged through the door and thrown into one of the collapsible chairs. The devil turned and locked the door behind him with the key from a length of thin, brown string around his neck.

Isaac Junior's eyes were ablaze with anger, but he was trying hard to hide the emotion behind a constructed wall of fear. He fell into the chair and quickly righted himself. He spun around to face his abuser so quickly that the action seemed choreographed. The child still blamed the robed devil for denying him a lifetime of supposed happiness and abundance from earlier that day.

Isaac Junior's torturer did not waste a moment. He had a habit of trying to break the spirit before breaking the body, but he was also skilled at doing both concurrently.

When he finally spoke, his voice was thick with contempt, each word sharpened to inflict damage. "So, you thought that man today would want *you*? A dumb, filthy, useless brat like *you*?"

"Yes. There is nothing wrong with me!" Isaac Junior replied at a volume that his captor was not expecting. His determination was strong but, at only 10 years old, his emotions were stronger. "What did you say to him?" he demanded through an onslaught of tears.

The devil was a little bemused by the outburst. "What did I *say* to him?" he smirked. "Well, nothing really. I just told him what your filthy mother said to me when she brought you here."

Isaac Junior could see right through the robed devil's strategy and found himself wondering how clever the man was. Past visits had simply been brutal physical assaults. Isaac Junior had prepared himself for bruises but not this type of attack.

"My mother was not filthy!" Isaac Junior spat, his body shaking. He had never been given any information about his mother or how he came to the orphanage. He certainly didn't know that his mother had not lived to see his birth. The boy, remembering the second statement and keen for any information at all, asked, "Anyway, what did she say?"

"Who? Your mother?" He paused to take a small delight in the child's misery. "Oh, I remember the day that filthy whore brought you in here. She said that you were the ugliest baby she had ever seen and that she never wanted to lay eyes on you again."

Isaac Junior sobbed. "No, she didn't! My mother was *beautiful*, and she *loved* me!" Although he was pleading against these words, he would carry their weight throughout his lifetime.

His tormentor was enjoying himself now. "Yes. I remember when she came into this very room. She sat in that very chair!" He pointed to Isaac Junior's seat. 'I told her, 'You don't want to leave him here.' I told her, 'Bad things happen to children here.' I told her, 'I will do bad things to him here.' And you know what she said?"

Isaac Junior's innocence was rapidly draining from his face. Externally, he looked defeated, but Isaac knew that he was finding his new self.

Isaac Junior's tiny voice had lost all its demand. "What did she say?"

The devil's eyes narrowed, his voice slowed, and he delivered the words like a venomous snake bite in slow motion: "She told me that she didn't care. She didn't love you and never wanted to see you again. She said that you belonged to me now and that I could do whatever I wanted with you. That's what I told that man today. Nobody wants you, and you belong to me."

At the same time, Isaac Junior and Isaac yelled, *"No, I don't!"*

Isaac had been so engrossed in the narrative playing out in front of him that he had forgotten how disconnected with this part of his life he had become. In that single moment of agony and defiance, he had become one with the child.

Isaac Junior jumped to his feet, grabbing items from the desk and throwing them at the devil, who just laughed in response. Then Isaac Junior threw a heavy stapler with all the force he could muster, which cracked the devil's temple with a thud. It was David against Goliath, but the lucky throw had found a weakness in the armor. Although it only opened a small wound on the priest's forehead, its weight was waging a new war within the man's skull.

The devil's good humor evaporated in an instant. "You little cunt! I'm going to make you pay for that." His eyes were flared like an enraged bull struggling to find its feet. He blinked his dizziness away, steadying himself for attack.

Isaac and Isaac Junior knew that both child and captor would never walk out of that room alive. Even if Isaac Junior did make it out, the retribution from this devil would find him at some point from that day forward. With his mother's memory in tatters and any chance of escape seemingly gone, Isaac Junior had nothing left to lose. He was finished living in fear and didn't care if it killed him.

The child grabbed at the desk for whatever he could throw — hole punches, staple removers, pens, pencils, anything his little hands could find — but he was running out of options, and the items were getting smaller. The devil, who was sensing a lull in the activity, reached for the leather strap on the side of his desk. With it, he would reassert himself as the apex predator within moments. The stricken boy followed his eyeline and lashed out to get there first. He pushed the paper trays and the leather strap onto the floor.

"As God is my witness, you will pay dearly for this, boy," the priest shouted as he leaned over the front of his chair to search the ground for his leather strap, which was now buried in the chaos of disheveled stationery.

Isaac Junior's surprised enthusiasm for this fight had caught him off guard, but the fight within him would have its limits. Now standing, he put the palms of both hands on the end of the desk and tried with all his might to topple it on the robed devil.

"The bookshelf!" Isaac screamed to his tiny self.

For the briefest moment, the child stopped. A casual observer might not have noticed, but it happened. Isaac Junior turned his chin slightly to the left as if having heard the command or at the very least considering his own new option.

Taking care not to get too close to the devil, Isaac Junior took a run at the pine bookshelf against the wall.

Still scouring the ground, the devil reached out to grab the child by the leg. His fingers clamped like vines around the boy's ankle. Isaac Junior kicked with all his might, but he was caught.

In the way that one might scream at a horror movie they had seen too many times before, Isaac screamed, "The bookshelf! The bookshelf!"

Fella's voice came over his shoulder. "He cannot hear you, Mr. McGlynn."

Luckily the child *did* react.

Instead of looking down at his captured leg, Isaac Junior surrendered to his fate and looked at the bookshelf with its many rows of religious volumes. With his tiny fingers, he grabbed at the crack between the back of the bookshelf and the wall, but it was too heavy to budge. Instead, he pulled at one of the biggest books on the top shelf and threw it at the back of the devil's head, but it was not enough.

The devil found the leather strap among the debris on the ground and caressed it between his fingers. A smile forced its way onto his face. His body found its strength, and he started to raise himself once again.

Before the devil had raised his second knee, Isaac Junior was on him. He grabbed multiple books and brought them down on his attacker. Some of the books found their target on the priest's shoulder and neck, but they only stalled him for a moment. The boy again worked his fingers into the space between the back of the bookshelf and the wall.

This time, without some of the larger books at the top, it moved slightly. It rocked in the devil's direction but not enough to topple over. When it righted itself on the back-swing, it crushed the boy's fingers against the wall. Isaac

Junior screamed in pain but didn't allow himself to lose focus. When the bookshelf rocked forward again, the boy pushed it with all his might. This time, the momentum carried it to an extreme edge, and the books began to fall.

Isaac Junior, with anxious sweat all over his body, pushed and screamed to release the air within his lungs and the power in his arms. The bookshelf fell past the tipping point like a majestic tree would fall in a forest —slow, heavy, determined — and released a roar. Not quite the groan of breaking wood, but the metallic scream of nails bending and straining under the weight of the fall.

The robed devil started to rise, holding the prized leather strap defiantly in his hand. He had been more focused on the strap than the bookshelf, which now loomed over him like a dark cloud. In that instant, Isaac Junior backed up to escape the arch of the fall.

The back of the devil's head caught the top lip of the bookshelf at full impact. Both Isaacs watched in anticipation. It was impossible to tell if the unnatural thud they heard emanated from the wood or the skull. Either way, the damage was done.

The bookshelf crashed to the floor, sending its remaining contents in all directions while crushing the priest's body. The room was almost silent.

Isaac Junior stared down at the carnage in front of him, still in fight mode, his breath heaving from the exertion and his muscles flexed for action. Noise, screaming, crying, pleading and general ruckus from this room had never garnered attention from the outside world in the past, and this room held its secrets once again.

After forty-five counted heartbeats and pure silence outside of his heavy breathing, Isaac Junior allowed himself to blink and regroup. He allowed his breathing to loosen in his chest and his shoulders to recall their natural position.

Never expecting the situation to progress this far, Isaac Junior looked confused. He had to consider his next step and, turning back to the room for answers, he saw no easy options. His only plan when he came into the room had been complete defiance, even if it meant his own life. The child simply wanted to make the devil pay for what he'd done. He never expected to stand over a limp body hemmed down by a bookshelf.

Isaac Junior picked up the chair he'd knocked over when jumping to his feet, as if getting in trouble for making a mess would be his worst crime. He was about to move for the door when he heard a guttural groan.

Bloodied hands appeared and found their purchase on the bookshelf as it slid sideways in its arch over the man's back. When his face finally appeared, it resembled a different person. There was blood from the top of his skull to the back of his head. As he straightened his back on his hands and knees, blood trickled down his cheeks.

The eyes of the devil searched for the boy and, through their haze, found him. After taking a breath, he threatened the boy with each word sounding like a challenge. "I am going to hurt you and hurt you and hurt you again until you are dead."

Isaac Junior looked around wildly for something to finish the job. At his feet was a stone plaque. The child bent down, picked it up and crossed the floor.

The devil, still blinking away his blood and concussion, did not see this act and had not finished his threats. He took another breath and found a fuller voice. "I will make you wish that you were never born, you little fuck! I will ... I will ..."

He paused as the boy's shadow appeared over him.

The priest lifted his hand above his head, but it was already too late. "No, *please* ..." he begged.

As Isaac watched this scene, he found irony in the devil's last words. These were the same two words that Isaac had sought so enthusiastically from all his victims through the years.

Isaac Junior showed the same level of mercy as he swung at the devil's head with all his might. The first blow landed but fell instead on the side of the priest's head with the shoulder taking the main impact. It was effective enough to take a significant amount of energy out of the man but not finish him. The devil's arms, which he had raised in self-defense, were now out of the equation.

Isaac Junior raised the stone plaque once again. This time, he would not stop until the job was done. The next three blows landed on the crown of the devil's head before the child allowed himself one breath to recover. The physical weight of the object was taking its toll on both of them. He then raised his tiny, shaking arms again and landed another three blows for good measure. When he finally dropped the plaque to the ground, all the ridges of the rock on it had been filled with blood, hair or brain matter.

Isaac Junior had only needed the first set of blows because, by the second set of three, the devil was already dead. Isaac could see this quite clearly although he was unsure if this was a new gift or if he would have seen it if he had been standing there alive.

As the devil's body absorbed each of the final blows, it shifted slightly before its final resting place, which just happened to align its eyes directly on the area of the room where Isaac was watching. On the third blow of the first set of three, at precisely the moment before the priest died, his eyes widened briefly in Isaac's direction. It was as if the devil had just realized that he had not been alone in the room with the boy.

The priest extinguished completely. Without their inner poison and rage, his eyes almost looked sad. There would be no pity for the devil that day.

Isaac soul was in turmoil. It was not easier or more satisfying the second time around, even though he was merely a voyeur. Having had the eyes of the devil settle on him in that final moment had turned him from witness to participant, which he had not been prepared for. He was stunned.

"He saw me!" Isaac said to Fella.

Fella responded immediately. "No! He saw a *premonition* of you, and you saw a *recording* of him. You were not dead when he was alive. It is important to remember that."

"I don't understand. What's the difference?"

"This is difficult to explain. Sometimes, when living people are close to death, they can see our side and glimpse many things. These details are not important right now and will keep you from focusing on what's in front of you. It is important that you watch."

* * *

Back in the orphanage office, Isaac Junior tried to comprehend the dead body in front of him. He lowered himself to make direct eye contact, just to be sure. He carefully placed the plaque on the floor and waved his hands in front of the

dead man's face. The body didn't react. When he was satisfied that there was no further threat from within the room
and that nobody was coming from the outside, Isaac Junior
allowed himself a moment to absorb the scene.

These images would become fodder for nightmares for the
rest of Isaac's life.

Isaac Junior knelt down closer to the body. He felt no fear
even though his face was only about sixteen inches from the
bloodied mess of the devil.

Isaac Junior drew every detail into his memory: the broken
fragments of bone; the slow drip of cortex blood; the thick,
hot smell of smashed brain. He used all his senses to perform one last act of defiance over this foe. He superimposed
this new broken image of the devil with the old face he had
come to fear and hate so intensely. He commended himself
for doing this job so thoroughly that it would be thirty years
and his own death before he would see that undamaged face
clearly once again.

Isaac Junior reached down and retrieved the door key from
the dead man's neck. He stood up and unlocked the door before
replacing the key to its original location. Taking great care not
to step in the blood on the floor, he silently left the room.

* * *

Catching Isaac off guard, Fella asked, "Did you get the closure you wanted, Mr. McGlynn?"

"I got it the first time around. Are you trying to make me
feel guilty? All I saw was a frightened child, trying to defend
himself against a man who had beaten and molested him for
years."

"No. I am not trying to make you feel guilty," Fella replied. "It is not my place to judge. This is your lifetime. We are simply watching the highlight reel so you can understand yourself better." Fella's voice softened as if whispering through a smile. "And, perhaps, there might still be a few surprises for you along the way."

* * *

At that moment, the door to the office opened an inch before a child's hand behind it retracted into the darkness. After it was deemed to be safe, Susan Junior poked her head around the edge of the door. Wide eyed, she took in the scene and turned back outside. When she was satisfied that she was alone and without threat, she silently entered the room like a mouse scurrying through a crack in a wall.

"My god!" Isaac said. "Susan knew?"

"Yes," Fella replied.

Susan Junior was older than last time but no taller. Her body would fulfill its absolute potential in her late teens. Many years later, her beauty would sting the eyes of those she targeted.

She crossed the room, skipping over the dead man but never taking her eyes from him. Always positioning herself just outside of his grasp, she climbed and stood on his desk. She opened a high cupboard, which had been the cause of many teary eyes over the years. In it, among all the toys and prized possessions taken from children, she pulled out a doll in the form of a young girl in a short, floral green skirt. Susan Junior regarded it again before reaching up the doll's dress and opening a hidden flap on its belly. She retrieved something from it and clutched it with her small fingers.

Isaac found it hard to believe that he remembered the doll but not its owner, even after all these years. He moved himself closer to get a look at what she had retrieved.

Susan Junior quickly glanced at the body on the floor and then carefully placed the doll on the table behind her. She unfolded the contents of its belly in her hands and turned it over.

Isaac saw a black-and-white photo of a young girl, perhaps sixteen or seventeen years old, who had a slight resemblance to the Susan whom he would one day come to know in adulthood. The style of the photo and its familiar background told Isaac that it had been cut from a group photo taken at the same orphanage.

Susan Junior smiled and clutched the photo between her thumbs and forefingers, pressing it to her lips. She refolded the photo and placed it back into the doll's belly. She hugged it tightly and was about to get down, but she stopped. She reached back in the drawer and withdrew Isaac Junior's brown bear and John Junior's truck. Taking all three items with her, she stepped around the body and closed the door behind her, being careful not to get blood on her feet, leaving the room as silently as she had entered.

As he watched, Isaac recalled finding his bear at the foot of his bed the following day.

Isaac Junior had spent two minutes wondering where it came from before deciding that perhaps God had been happy with him for his actions the night before or that he simply didn't care who brought it. That morning, there would be more pressing matters at hand.

Burning the Past to Feed the Future

ISAAC FOUND HIMSELF BACK IN the vacuum of space, but this time there was no dancing ball of light. Just black, everywhere. Finding himself with no focal point and no physical body left him feeling disorientated. He tried to imagine where the tips of his fingers extended, but the visual image rolled back in his mind. It left him with the feeling that, even though his space seemed limitless in this new world, there was not enough room for imagination. He could not even get a sense of the skull that housed his brain where these thoughts must be originating. Once again, the vision did not stick but instead rolled in on itself.

"I have no body," Isaac thought. "But, if I can think these thoughts, I must exist. So now, I must think!"

* * *

Isaac let his mind drift back to where he had just left off. This time there was no virtual reality, no holy rewind. Just good, old-fashioned memory.

He recalled the late-night trip back to his dormitory room, passing the sleeping children. To the best of his knowledge, none of them had been concerned with his safety that night. In the orphanage, the only time one had been able to truly sleep soundly was when they knew that Brother Anthony had selected someone else for the night. Most of the time, it didn't matter who it was, just as long as it hadn't been you.

Isaac recalled climbing into his bed that night and hearing John call him from his bed, which was jumping distance away. John had always been his one exception to everything.

Isaac remembered holding up his trembling hand to stop John from making any further noise. There had been just enough light for them to pick out each other's forms and basic gestures but not features. Isaac had held his forefinger to his mouth and pointed to the room, making it clear that he didn't want anyone to wake up and see that he had not been in bed. John had nodded and rolled over. Isaac remembered hearing the familiar sound of John's snoring within seconds.

Isaac recalled the morning following the death of Brother Anthony. The children had woken to a sea of faces they did not recognize. Police officers and ambulance staff had walked to and from the priest's office all morning. Men and women in suits had tried to decide what to do with the children now in their care. All the other brothers and sisters who ran the orphanage had gathered together, with concern and a little guilt painted on their faces. One by one, they had been led into the library to be interviewed by police. Isaac recalled that no child had ever been questioned about the event.

* * *

Years later, Isaac would learn from a retired policeman that, upon searching the crime scene, the detectives had uncovered many compromising photos and documents in Brother Anthony's office. The policeman had refused to give any more information about the content of the photos but confessed that there may have been high-ranking government officials and small children involved. Isaac had guessed that these photos were kept to either blackmail the perpetrators or simply for Brother Anthony's personal gratification.

The officers had been instructed by their superiors, who were desperate to make the scandal go away. They had called it "an accident with an off-balance bookshelf" and had wound up the investigation as fast as possible. Within a week, all the children had been relocated.

* * *

Isaac recalled that the local community had been rife with rumors about the orphanage and, feeling a little guilty that these heinous crimes had occurred in their neighborhood, the community had responded. It had started with one of the city's elite families coming forward to adopt a child. Soon, it was considered the right thing to do. Families had come forward and adopted the orphanage children like it was part of their civil code, albeit a code that had not been in their DNA while the children had suffered before. The few children who weren't taken by sympathetic families had been relocated out of state to another orphanage, which had been rapidly expanded to accommodate the new arrivals.

Isaac had been one of the lucky ones. In earlier days at the orphanage, Isaac had noticed a kind, older couple. He found out that they never had children of their own and wanted a child just like they were. Isaac had played up to them once or twice before. Then, after the death of Brother Anthony, they had taken the bait. Isaac's skin and hair color helped his cause because it was the same as theirs, and he looked as if he could be a blood relation.

The adoption process would have progressed without a hitch had Isaac not insisted that he and John were brothers and needed to be kept together. The two boys did not look alike, but the elderly couple were already committed to Isaac and had decided to indulge his request.

Although it was a full adoption, neither boy had ever fully belonged to their new parents. The two boys had been their own people and not part of a ready-made family. They had been sympathetic to those who housed and fed them, supportive of each other and a menace to anyone who got in their way.

* * *

In their new family home and with the new array of quality food being brought to the dining table each night, the boys had thrived. Their lean skeletons had clung to this nourishment and, in a few months, both had found their bodies repaired from the damages inflicted at the orphanage. And, while Isaac had caught his new parents peering at his scars, the topic of their torment at the hands of Brother Anthony had never been discussed.

The boys had grown strong. Within six months, the ability to intimidate their school peers had rarely required any violence. Their reputations and physical presence had been enough for them to get whatever they — or at least Isaac— wanted. However, they had never been completely heartless. If other kids had nothing of value or were prepared to give up what they did have peacefully, it was a safe place for all.

Thinking back, Isaac commended himself for never wielding violence unless necessary. And, when all else failed, it had been done ruthlessly.

Both boys had also attained excellent academic marks, especially in mathematics. Isaac had chosen this field as their specialty to help them with their future financial success. However, survival for the brothers had always required brain as well as brawn, and Isaac did not want to let either suffer in their new world. Whenever John had fallen behind in his studies, Isaac had ordered him to study and sat with him while he did it. Isaac had made sure that his own grades had never fallen.

* * *

Isaac's final memory of his childhood was the day it had officially ended. A few weeks after Isaac's assumed eighteenth birthday, he had summonsed John and their adoptive parents to a family meeting. The orphanage had lost reference to the correct dates of both his and John's birthdays, but they had known the year. The family had simply celebrated on the anniversary of their adoption.

Isaac recalled every word of his little speech:

"Jason and Colette, John and I firstly want to thank you both for adopting us when you did. I can appreciate that, having had no children of your own, it was difficult to take us both on," he said as he smiled.

Their adoptive parents had looked at each other and smiled politely, wondering where the conversation was heading.

"You both did a fine job, given the circumstances. However, I want to let you know that we've got it from here. We will be moving out on Friday. You might not see us again. We are moving on."

Isaac recalled that John had shifted uncomfortably in his seat after hearing the news, but he had said nothing. He had not been consulted beforehand.

Jason and Colette had looked at each other, Isaac remembered, unable to voice the unknown word they both seemed to be searching for. The boys' characters had been no secret to them, and they may have even guessed that this day would come. Now that it had arrived, the expectation had not made it any easier.

"I assure you that neither of you have done anything wrong," Isaac had continued, "and that our lives here were a pleasure after what we both suffered at the orphanage. It is simply time for us to move forward, and we can't do that looking back."

* * *

The brightness in the vacuum of space flickered like someone had just switched on a heavenly tungsten light. The light flashed three times before it took hold and Isaac's world was illuminated. Once again, the bodily misaligned Fella stood in front of him.

Fella looked confused and asked. "You finally got the chance to have a family, and you pushed them away?"

Isaac didn't want to address this question directly, so he

countered with one of his own. "Are they here, Fella? Are they part of the Many Many?"

"No, Mr. McGlynn. They are old, but they have each other, so they cling to their lives desperately. They still search your photos for the happiness you and John once brought them and since took away."

"They were good people, Fella, I told them that. I made my life real, not them. They were not there when I suffered at the hands of Brother Anthony and his friends. They were not there when I took his life and felt his blood and brain between my fingers. They should have gotten to me before that day! Perhaps things may have been different."

Fella pondered Isaac's response and paused to take an internal counsel. Finally, he seemed to accept either his own thoughts or what he was being told and asked, "So, Mr. McGlynn, are you ready?"

"Ready for what?"

"Are you ready to join us? Are you ready to become part of the Many Many?"

"Is *he* in there, Fella? Would I be thrust back into another world with *him*? I will kill him again if I can. I still hate him. If he is in there, then I hate the Many Many."

Fella was visually disturbed and confused by Isaac's response. "If you hate him, it is like hating the ocean because of a single drop of poison splashed into its waves. We are both abuser and abused. Alongside the bad, your biological mother and many amazing souls are in here also. Does the overwhelming good not outweigh the bad?"

"Maybe, but I had my life taken from me. I'm not ready to have my death taken from me also," Isaac responded indignantly.

"Good. I was hoping you would say that," Fella said. "Are you ready to become a witness for the living then?"

Isaac thought for a moment before replying. He knew that moving on was going to be a big step in his evolution — or whatever this part of his death was called.

"No, I'm not ready yet, Fella. I need one last thing from you."

One Last Rewind

"NO! IT IS NOT POSSIBLE," Fella said flatly, already knowing what Isaac needed.

Isaac laughed. It was the first time he had ever heard Fella without a melodic ring to his voice. "We are in heaven! Surely *anything* is possible. Whom do I need to talk to?" He had been told "no" many times in his life, but it had never stopped him.

Fella's mood did not improve. "There is nobody to talk to, Mr. McGlynn. Just me and the Many Many. And I am telling you that it is not possible."

Isaac was not ready to give up yet. He needed to find an angle that he could use to his advantage. "Why is that, Fella? Why is it so difficult to give me one more rewind of my own life before I move on to whatever is next?"

"Because you have used up all your rewind time. I warned you that it was running short, but you wasted it reliving your vengeance. It seems that your conquests are more important than your happiness. A life is created in moments, Isaac McGlynn. You focused on the wrong moments."

"How can you judge me? How long has it been since you lived? It was *my* life to live. The moments that created me chose me just as much as I chose them! What is it going to cost me to relive this one last moment? I have money! I brought it with me."

Fella's face grew red with an unnatural rage. 'Your money is *worthless* here! We are all equal in heaven."

Isaac didn't miss a beat. "Good. Then I am at least equal. I'm not trying to be difficult. This is important to me, and I have something that you don't. Let me share it so we are all equal again. I just want one more rewind to put my life behind me with all the blanks filled in. I need to see what I missed the day I met Susan in my office for the first time."

Fella shook his head and was about to respond before he completely froze. To Isaac, it looked like a computer glitch, a frozen screen waiting to come back to life in mid animation.

"Fella, are you with me?"

Fella sprung to life again. "The Many Many are talking to me, Isaac McGlynn. Some are happy to relieve you of the money that you wasted so much of your life on. One has agreed to give you some of his remaining rewind time in exchange for your money."

"Great! It seems that, even in heaven, deals can be done." Isaac was satisfied but wondered if he should negotiate an exact figure. Then he realized that he had no idea how much money he had.

"Sometimes deals can be done, Mr. McGlynn, but not in the way that you think. You only just got here. Don't be so sure that you know how this place works."

* * *

Immediately, the light source was extinguished once again, and Isaac was floating within the blackness of space without stars. It seemed to happen faster than a light switch and without the faint afterglow of a bulb. Pure light to pure black in an instant. The sparkling ball of light was back, although something about it was unfamiliar. Perhaps it was a distinct color or warmth. Isaac wasn't sure, but he felt that he was using someone else's magic this time.

When the light expanded to engulf him on the third pass, his new world was rich, appearing at once in full, living color. In fact, it was an *excess* of color. His real-world office had never looked this good. Isaac took the entire scene into his vision. He was convinced that he saw colors that never existed while he was on Earth, but he was unable to pinpoint them.

Fella could sense his wonder. "You could have seen the world like this, Mr. McGlynn. It is the price you paid for the pain you suffered and the life you took. There is always a price to pay for death, regardless of how justified you may feel."

"I have *always* been prepared to pay for what I want, Fella. It was worth it."

While the background scene rendered itself quickly, the people in it were slower to materialize. The first was a slightly younger version of himself, sitting in the chair behind his desk. John Senior was sitting directly across from him. Once they had both been rendered, the scene burst into activity and the normal flow of time carried them once again within its current.

"We may need to pass around the hat to the usual suspects once again," Isaac Senior said to John Senior.

The men's investments were performing well, and they

were about to embark on another wave of growth. This step would require more backing from their core investors.

Isaac Senior leaned forward across the desk. "You need to remind them just how much fucking money we have made them this year. If they want it to continue, they need to invest more!"

John Senior nodded, accustomed to his role of money collector. "And what if our good friend wants to withdraw his investment once again?"

"If he says one single word outside of 'please take my fucking money,' remind him of the great working relationship we have shared together … and that I will have you break his legs if he asks again."

John Senior smiled. It had been so long since he'd gotten his hands dirty. Business suits never fit him the way they fit Isaac.

Isaac Senior's phone buzzed. "Yep?"

It was Ava, his executive assistant. The whiny sound of her voice ran a fingernail down Isaac Senior's spine. "I have your eleven am here. She's just your type."

"Send her in," Isaac Senior replied, having no idea what his "eleven am" actually was. He returned his attention to John Senior. "You know what you need to do?"

John Senior got up from his chair "Yep."

"We need another three million," Isaac Senior said, finally looking back to the papers on his desk. Without looking up, he pointed at the door. "Go now. Go do what you do best!"

John Senior took the two steps for the door. As he reached for the handle, it opened from the other side. It would be the first of thousands of times that John and Susan would cross paths across the threshold of that office.

John Senior gave her an awkward smile that men often did in her presence. "Hi" was all he could bring himself to say.

On seeing her perfection again, Isaac lost himself. He took a breath that his heavenly body didn't need and held it longer than any living person possibly could.

Susan Senior acknowledged John Senior with a nod but was saving her words for Isaac Senior, who had not yet looked up from his desk. She crossed the room silently like a cat stalking its prey.

John Senior hesitated at the door, just long enough to watch her walk all the way to the desk and stand there, waiting for Isaac Senior's attention. He smiled to himself and shut the door. "I hope she can type," he said under his breath before chuckling and walking back to his desk.

Back in the room, Susan Senior still had not said a word, and Isaac Senior still had not looked up from the paperwork on his desk. She stood with the posture of an athlete and the confidence of a statesman. Her dress was the color of a blood rose and fitted her with respect. She waited silently.

In the rewind, Isaac studied her thoroughly, even if his other self paid her no attention. Her eyes gave away no secrets. If she recognized Isaac Senior from the orphanage, she wasn't showing it. She simply stood there, smiling politely. She let her eyes wander around Isaac Senior, scanning his desk, his cupboards and even his clothes. Isaac knew that she was filing it all away in case she needed to use it later.

After a painfully slow forty-five seconds of inactivity, Isaac Senior finally caught a glimpse of Susan Senior's dress out of the corner of his eye. He had been so engrossed in what he was reading that he had forgotten he was expecting company.

As he turned his head to see what was in front of him, Isaac Senior was caught completely off guard. Startled, he jumped back in his chair, almost knocking it over. He found Susan Senior's face, and his surprise turned to awe at her beauty.

* * *

Isaac McGlynn always bought the best. However, among all the women he had met or who had served him, there had been something missing. They were all too perfect. Their faces were a folded mirror of geometric perfection. With Susan, it was different.

Her imperfections were a celebration of beauty itself. The slight gap in her front teeth. The way that her right eye probed your soul. The slight sadness behind her smile. Each and every imperfection told its own story. Isaac wasn't sure why, but he had a strong sense that she had been handcrafted by an artisan in his prime, especially for Isaac.

* * *

"Hello," Susan Senior said quietly, as if the message was only for him in a crowded room. "I'm Susan."

"How long have you been standing there?" Isaac Senior asked, unsure how it was possible that he did not sense her presence.

"Since John left," she replied through a smile.

If Isaac Senior had been paying attention, he may have found it interesting that she knew John Senior's name even though they had not been introduced.

"Why didn't you interrupt me?" Isaac Senior asked sincerely.

"Because my job, if you hire me as your assistant, is to support you with whatever you need. If I'm interrupting you from doing your job, of what value would I be?"

Isaac Senior could already tell that this was not going to be a *standard* job interview.

Isaac watched Susan and himself from heaven in amazement. Although he had not noticed the change at the time, the man sitting in front him was not the one there only moments ago.

Isaac Senior pointed to the chair in front of him. "Please sit," he said without the pretense one might show a stranger. There was no polite smile like on Susan Senior's face. He was suddenly approaching this meeting as if he were about to make the biggest decision of his life. "Tell me about yourself."

"My name is Susan Mitchell. I'm here to replace Ava."

Isaac Senior was taken aback by her frankness. No one had ever come for an interview with so much directness. That was *his* role.

"Where was your last job?" he asked, trying to remind her that it was an interview.

"Where I came from before doesn't matter, Mr. McGlynn. If you don't judge me for my history, then I won't judge you. What matters is that I'm here now. And that I work for you."

Being an orphan, albeit one who was adopted, Isaac Senior was no stranger to distancing himself from his history. He felt no desire to test her on it specifically, but there would need to be a test of some sort. Service to him was never enough. No matter how beautiful this woman was, he would require absolute proof of devotion.

Isaac Senior sat back in his chair and allowed the time to pass. Susan Senior smiled and said nothing. She was not being called on for information, so she did not bother him with it. She held his eye contact the entire time without wavering.

Finally, after what seemed like an eternity to each of them, Isaac Senior leaned forward. "I want you to go outside and fire Ava. I want you to help her pack her things into a box and walk her out of the building within fifteen minutes. Do you understand?"

"Yes," Susan Senior said with a polite smile. Her face was devoid of any judgment or emotion. She stood to leave the room.

"And Susan, I don't care what she says or how sad or angry she gets. She does not get through that door again. Understood?"

"Clearly understood," she replied, again with a nonjudgmental smile.

"When you finish doing that, come back to me and lock the door. You are about to have an uncomfortable afternoon. If you make it through today, I may just offer you the opportunity of a lifetime. However, if any of this frightens you, then open the door and just keep walking."

Susan Senior smiled again, a little wider this time. "I'll be back in fifteen minutes."

It was not often that Isaac surprised himself, but he did on that day. He could not recall ever requesting a new assistant. He had made a mental note to ask her about it. However, in all the time they had shared together, he never did. Thinking back on it now, perhaps he was scared of what the potential answer might be.

* * *

From the moment that Susan Mitchell entered Isaac's office that day, her fate entangled with that of Isaac McGlynn and John Hannebery like three strands of a rope. Each enforced the strength of the other, and together there was nothing they could not accomplish.

Isaac spoke over his right shoulder. "Fella, I am done here now. I don't want to see anymore."

"Why stop now, Mr. McGlynn? Don't you want to relive all the details of your afternoon with Susan and your infamous agreement? After all, as they say, the devil is in the detail."

"Do you think that I wanted to come here to relive my old conquests? You're very wrong, Fella. I'm here to face my shame. Dealing in money is one thing, but I should never have treated Susan the way I did that day."

"As I said earlier, Mr. McGlynn, we don't know you very well. You have been in the dark to us, and we are doing our best to learn about you as we go along."

"Well, know this: I tried to rip up that stupid contract three times, but Susan wouldn't let me. She kept her copy bound like a trophy. She said that it wasn't about the money."

"Then what *was* it about?"

"I don't know. I was hoping to find out."

With that statement, Isaac McGlynn's world went black once again. This time, he did not have to wait in the darkness for long.

Back to the Present

———◆———

ISAAC FOUND OUT THAT HEAVEN was not a precise machine. Sometimes rewinds and transitions worked instantly; with others, he had to wait for things to render like an unpredictable internet connection to reality. This time, the blackness of space turned slowly but surely into white. All Isaac could do was wait out the fifty shades in between.

When he finally got to the shade of white where he had physical form and could actually talk, Fella presented himself to Isaac once again. "You are a complex man, Mr. McGlynn. We are never quite sure that we know what you are going to say next." Fella nodded, indicating to Isaac that, in a world where they saw almost everything, this statement should be considered a compliment.

"As you just saw, Fella, sometimes I don't know myself." Then he changed the mood to a lighter one. "So, since that was my last rewind, where do we go from here?"

"Well, we can't indulge your nostalgia anymore. The lifetime of Isaac McGlynn is over. At this point, no amount of pleading or money is going to change that. They have made this clear to me, and I am passing the message to you. Now, if they will have you, are you ready to join the Many Many?"

"No!" Isaac said defiantly. "I gave up my life, but I'm not ready to give up my death!"

"So, the next step is your choice. We don't want the living to suffer as you did."

Isaac shuffled a little, unsure of which suffering Fella was referring to.

Fella continued. "Every life needs validation. Like the proverbial tree falling in the forest, we must observe humanity for it to be. Your job now is to become a witness for the living. The only choice is whom you would like to observe first."

It was a simple question to Isaac on the face of things, but the decision was not immediate. "There are only two people alive whom I care about. I have been looking after one my whole life, and I hardly know the other at all." It was a battle between responsibility and intrigue, so Isaac did what he had always done — whatever pleased him. "Susan," he said quietly. "I want to see Susan first."

"So be it, Mr. McGlynn. Remember: It's not about you anymore. This next phase of your death may be more difficult than you think," Fella said before disappearing.

Isaac called after him. "And what about you, Fella? What will *you* do now?"

Fella's voice whispered directly into his ears as if he had just crept up behind Isaac. "I'll be watching you. For like the living without you, you without me are just a whisper in the wind."

* * *

A new world superimposed itself on the one in front of Isaac, which made him wonder for a brief moment where heaven was located. He had not dropped from a height or risen from the floor, so it was hard to get a perspective. Instead, he had been dialed in to a new reality like changing channels on a TV.

Instead of just viewing it, Isaac was now in a room he did not recognize and was quite sure he had never been in before. It was a large, open-space room with soaring ceilings and exposed beams. It had all the hallmarks of a self-contained loft apartment but owned by someone with expensive, minimalist taste. Everything visible served a function, and Isaac could not see a single item with a sole purpose of decoration.

And, while his recent rewinds had their own color scheme, this new living world had a vibrancy all its own. It was not a faded picture of the past. It was the brightly illuminated present. Isaac was back in the land of the living, and it seemed that the world had been given an upgrade while he was away. If the rewinds were analog, then this was digital.

Isaac heard a key rattle in the front door of the apartment. Even though he had no physical body and was in someone else's living space, his first instinct was to hide.

When the door swung open, everything made sense. Susan walked in, casually throwing her keys on a table designed for such a purpose. Her handbag was tossed on a chocolate brown couch, which still didn't show creases from regular use. She was wearing the same clothes as when Isaac died.

After taking three steps into her apartment, and with the door safely closed, Susan kicked off her heels, surrendering almost an inch and a half in height. She collected the shoes in her hands and headed for the bedroom.

Isaac followed at what he could only guess was a safe distance.

"How is it that I've never been to her place?" Isaac said aloud. He had certainly summonsed her to his apartment many times, but he had never been invited here.

When Isaac entered Susan's bedroom, two things immediately struck him as strange.

At first glance, it seemed as if she had a hospital bed. On further inspection and because Isaac had spent so much time in them recently, he knew that it wasn't. A hospital bed would allow a patient to sit up. This bed was completely flat with a minimal foam mattress. Isaac was sure that it was the cheapest piece of furniture in the entire loft. This was an institutional bed, similar to the bunks at the orphanage. With all the splendid refinery that had gone into creating the modern Susan, it seemed to Isaac that her sleeping preferences had not matured in the slightest. Seeing it made him shiver, and a wave of shame came over him for his own former luxuries.

The other item that struck Isaac as strange was her clothes. They were not safely stored away in a closet like any other modern bedroom. Instead, Susan's clothes were separated onto a small bed table for her personal items and a standing rack of clothes across the back of the room like a stage actress might keep for an evening show's costumes.

Isaac allowed himself to drift down the rack, allowing each of his favorite dresses to remind him of their past glories. Some of the clothes still had their labels attached. They would release their secrets to others in the living world, but he would now be relegated to voyeur.

At the end of the clothes rack, Isaac got his biggest surprise. Attached to the metal stand were three photos, all loosely stuck together with tape and obviously designed to be a quick reference guide. Isaac studied each of the photos briefly before shock hit him. He re-examined them to be absolutely sure of his suspicion.

In each photo was a different high-class escort whom Isaac had engaged with in the months preceding his first encounter with Susan inside his office. He couldn't be sure, but perhaps these photos were taken on the same days that he had been with them. Isaac calculated that, if this assumption were true, at least one photo was taken up to six months before he and Susan had met. As he considered the photos and the clothes, the similarities in the styles were clear.

The next thing Isaac noticed was how similar one of the girls — his favorite at the time — looked to Susan. Other than widely classifying both as his "type of woman," he had never once considered the comparison between the two. It made him wonder how much he had already desired of the Susan he knew before he died and how much had been crafted for him.

While Isaac's heavenly mind was being blown, Susan went about her business, undressing to her underwear, placing the day's dress into the clothing bin in her room and walking into her bathroom.

"Out of respect for you, Isaac, I wore your favorite dress today, but I won't wear it again," she said with a slightly different intonation to her voice than Isaac had been accustomed to hearing.

Isaac was a little surprised to be addressed directly but responded just in case Susan could hear him. "You always looked beautiful in that dress," he said to her and to no one.

As if she had heard him, she smiled and went about her business, removing her makeup.

Isaac resumed his position of voyeur behind Susan as she

stood in front of the mirror and addressed her face. Each swipe of her cotton pad removed the face he knew until a final soak of water and a last scrub revealed a face he didn't. The shape of her jaw was the same. The light at the back of her eyes still shone like the sun at dusk. Even her cheeks glowed with the color of the deepest pink rose. Although the face was the same behind the makeup, the woman was different.

Isaac took a hard look at her again to try and uncover the real Susan Mitchell. With her bare body now in full view — apart from a bra and panties — Isaac allowed his eyes to savor the experience, but something about his admiration was no longer the same. The sight of her no longer elicited the same physical reaction it once had. Her face, without eyeliner, no longer commanded the attention it had in the office. The new face he saw in front of him was a little more lost and fragile. He saw her now — not as a woman to be conquered but instead a normal human being, complete with disguises and insecurities. This frailty made her beautiful. Although he had known her for some time, he felt like he had witnessed her deconstruction and been given a peek behind the veil.

Again, as if she sensed his presence, Susan took a quick look around her bedroom before searching for herself once again in the mirror. She took a final, deep, introspective breath and said, "This is it, Isaac! It's all I am. I'm sorry if I disappointed you."

"Never!" Isaac replied to the room.

All Dressed Up and
Nowhere to Go

———•———

ISAAC SAT IN SILENCE WITH Susan for the next fifteen minutes before Fella was back in his ears once again.

"Mr. McGlynn, how are you finding your second life as a witness?"

Susan's life continued to play out in the background while Fella spoke, but it was now unfocused, as if looking through a frosted window.

"Is that what this is called? My second life?"

"Well, that's the interesting thing. There are many names for all the things that have happened to you since you were delivered to us. The experience will be of a similar nature after each death. However, the words that other souls may use to help the newly arrived deal with the situation may be different. As I mentioned earlier, I didn't recall my own name when you first got here. Names or descriptions don't really matter once you hit a certain point in your progression."

"Susan ..." Isaac started, "... seems to know that I'm here? She speaks to me."

"Is that so, Mr. McGlynn? Let me ask you this: Does she

speak to you because you are there, or are you there because she speaks to you?"

Isaac thought for a moment before responding. "How would I know? I thought *you* had all the answers."

Fella giggled. "To this question, we don't even know the answer, but it's fun to consider. We have a lot of answers in heaven. We even have answers that don't have questions! You think you are confused now!"

Isaac had a sudden flashback to old poltergeist movies he'd seen. "Can I move things?"

"No," Fella replied flatly, perhaps slightly insulted.

"If I can't make things move, what am I then?"

"You are the reason that humans exist, and they validate your existence in return. You are the breath on the back of their neck when danger is close and the warmth of the sun when they shake with cold. You are their witness and their guardian. And, Mr. McGlynn ..."

"Yes?"

"It is your privilege!"

Isaac scoffed. "This is becoming very frustrating."

"You are not in control here, Mr. McGlynn. Neither am I for that matter. The sooner you learn to accept that, the easier it will be for you."

* * *

The phone in Susan's apartment rang, and Isaac unfocused on Fella and brought the living back into his vision. He was surprised by his ability to do this for it had not been taught to him. He was learning new things instinctively.

Isaac watched as Susan looked at the phone's display. She

didn't recognize the number but chose to answer the call anyway.

"Yes?" she said flatly.

Isaac strained to hear the voice, which came though as if resonating from tin cans connected by string.

"Hello, Ms. Mitchell. I'm Sergeant Tony Papley," he said with a nasal twang. "Firstly, let me say that I am very sorry for your loss, ma'am."

Susan and John had prepared themselves for the possibility of a call like this and had prepared scripts. Should either prove unconvincing, Isaac had prearranged for their lawyer to be at their side within two hours. Their lawyer's guaranteed response service was designed to intimidate, overwhelm and delay any proceedings until the full force of the agency could arrive.

"Thank you, Officer Papley," Susan said, emphasizing his name with a little more of the accent that Isaac was familiar with. "You know, it's such a shame. He was a good man. Gave millions to charity, you know."

"I did not know that, ma'am. Again, I am sorry for your loss. We would have called his family, but he doesn't seem to have any?" He said this as more of a question than a statement.

"That's correct. You could say that John, his business partner, and I were as close to family as he got. Neither of us had family either, so I guess we all just fell together."

Susan offered more information than she was being asked. It was an attempt to show that she had nothing to hide. If the officer chose to check, he would not find anything out of order. They had developed this dialog with their lawyer before Isaac's death. Back then, Isaac had simply assumed that Susan's family was in some exotic country. He had never once thought to ask about them and hated himself for it now.

"Sorry, Officer Papley. I'm rambling. Was there something specific that I can help you with? It's been a big day," she added with an exhausted tone.

"No, ma'am. Well, not for today anyway. When a rich man dies, we just need to make sure that all the paperwork is in order. I will leave you with your grief for today. Maybe in a few days I could call on you again, just to fill in a few missing pieces."

The next step they had orchestrated for Susan was to test the level of interest in Isaac's death.

"Officer, if there are any issues, I'm happy to come over right now," Susan said innocently. "I'll just pull myself together and be there in an hour."

If he had said "yes," it would indicate a small hole in their planning. A "no" would likely mean that it was just a routine call. Their plan for "yes " included Susan arriving at the station, one of their best lawyers arriving forty-five minutes after that and another arriving every remaining hour that she was there. Legal representation by brute force.

"No, ma'am. That won't be necessary. It's mostly routine stuff here. Nothing that can't wait a few days," he replied sincerely enough for Isaac's liking. "In fact, I think we probably won't need to bother you further if you say that there was no family."

"Well, okay then. Why don't you give me your details? When things settle down here, I'll give you a call."

They exchanged information and hung up. Susan sent a text message with the details to the standby lawyer and returned to her bedroom to continue getting dressed.

* * *

Seeing Susan in her own surroundings, Isaac had an overwhelming desire to understand the woman he had taken for granted for years. For the first time, he swung his vantage point around her, taking her in from head to toe on all sides. It was the first time that his level of sight had shifted out of his normal living viewing height, and he found himself detaching from his old self. It was as if his eyes were floating in space now, and something about it gave him an incredible sense of freedom.

Fella's voice rang in his ears once again. "You have taken to this new station well, Mr. McGlynn. I am going to leave you now. If you have a question, you simply need to ask it and I will reply."

"Where will you go, Fella?"

"I need to return to the Many Many. I have some questions for their answers."

Isaac let out an exasperated gasp, and Fella's presence left the room. For the first time since his death, and with the living right in front of him, Isaac McGlynn felt utterly alone.

Once again, the phone rang. This time, its chime was one-part melody and one-part fingernails on a blackboard.

The Dark Call

———•———

SINCE THE LAST CALL, SUSAN had time to put on a tight pair of jeans with a light blue t-shirt. It was a simple cross between home-casual and down-time super model. It occurred to Isaac that he had never seen her dress so comfortably before.

She looked at the phone as it vibrated in her hands. She saw the name on the caller ID and took the call with a resolute self-assurance, which may have convinced her but not Isaac. He could not see the caller ID, but he knew that she did not want to take this call.

"Yes?" she said coldly, as if sucking on ice cubes.

"You never told me that he was dying!" said the unknown male voice aggressively. "If you think that this is going to get you out of the deal, then think again, bitch. I want my money!"

"Nothing has changed!" Susan replied quickly. "And his dying was none of your business. Our deal still stands. I pay the money, and you give me the photos." Her heavy breathing continued even after the words had finished. She was trying to match his anger.

"You bet your pretty little ass it does! I want that money in my hands by tomorrow."

"No!" Susan said firmly. "I told that you our deal still stands, so the existing terms still stand. I will have the money for you at the end of the week as we agreed. You have no need to panic. You still have something I want, and I will pay you for it. Believe me, the last thing you want to do right now is panic and do something stupid. You will lose it all ... and maybe more."

Isaac listened to the conversation in astonishment. He was jumping to seven conclusions at once and didn't understand any of them. He thought hard but could not recognize the voice on the phone.

The male caller's breath could be heard, heavy and controlled. "Okay. I am going to pretend that you didn't just threaten me, and we will continue with the original plan. You have the money for me by the end of the week. You get what you want, and we go our separate ways. I'll call you later in the week to discuss the details."

The line went dead, and Susan dropped the phone onto the bed.

Isaac considered this new Susan for a moment. She was scared and vulnerable, which were two emotions he had never seen cross her face before. Their shadow made a crack in her marble. If this man had been intimidating her while she worked for Isaac, he had never noticed it. Isaac always thought that he knew the majority of her, especially given their numerous physical encounters, but he was starting to realize that he may have only known one shaving of her soul.

Susan put her chin in the air, ran her fingers through her hair and shook off the call. "I wonder what the rich people are doing today?" she said ironically. Then she nodded in a fashion that seemed to say, "I had better go and find out!"

She grabbed one of the three sets of car keys now at her disposal. One of them belonged to her old Toyota, which she'd had for over five years. The other two were high-performance sports cars, which had recently been transferred from Isaac's garage days before his death. Each of them was worth more than her entire loft apartment. On this occasion, Susan chose the Aston Martin for her afternoon adventure.

She was out the door and on her way before the door had time to swing shut and self-lock.

Isaac followed her to the car, either one step behind or in front. As long as he kept Susan as his sole focus, he could pivot around her. It was as if he were tethered to her on a rope and was able to swing about her freely.

Once they were both in the car, Susan allowed herself a few moments to get familiar with the controls and her new dashboard.

Isaac had an idea about what was coming. When he drove his first sports car, the power of the machine had been completely intimidating. He expected Susan to struggle with the throttle, the gears and the steering.

She started the engine, and the car roared into action. A smile spread across her cheeks. She allowed herself one determined pump of the accelerator to tell the world that she would now be driving first class.

"We are in this together now," she said, either to the car or to Isaac. "If you don't make me look like a fool, I won't make you look like a fool." It was like making a pact with a raging bull. Susan was whispering in its ear, telling it that she meant it no harm. On this occasion, with the full seduction of her voice, the bull relented.

Riding with Susan was the smoothest trip Isaac had ever

had in that car. She harnessed the power of the throttle, transitioned through the gears and guided it through every turn like a professional. She pulled up to a valet parking section of an exclusive shopping mall and lifted herself out of the car.

Isaac thought, "The car belongs to her now. She has earned its trust and respect."

As she left the car in the parking lot, she ran a smooth hand across its back. "Good boy," she said, low and deep without a hint of sarcasm. She greeted the attendant with a smile, accepted her parking ticket and strode on without looking back.

* * *

It was the sort of mall that had its own people. If you had the money to transact here, then you were part of the club. If you didn't, you were an unwelcome tourist.

Susan allowed herself to walk freely among the people as if she had been there all her life. The only difference was that she was not yet dressed in the clothes of luxury like so many of those around her. She walked into the first shop that took her fancy.

"Hello, ma'am," the shop assistant said to Susan in a cool I-know-my-place tone. "Is there anything that I can help you with today?" She was a short, blonde woman dressed in the store uniform's dark suit.

Susan smiled. "I think I'm going to spoil myself today."

The shop assistant sized her up and noticed that Susan's attire was not what she was accustomed to from her other shoppers. "Is there anybody that you were hoping to impress?"

"Oh, no. They all have to impress me now!"

Susan spent her new money with abandon for the next four hours while Isaac watched. It was clear that her concern earlier that morning was based on her old financial status and that her spending habits were new. Isaac had never specifically noticed the quality of her garments before. However, in these new clothes — these works of art — he could see that Susan had hit a whole new level of sophistication. While in the presence of these new people of means, she had resorted to the high-class accent she had used in front of Isaac over the previous three years, but its resonance rang truer in these closes. She was one of them right before his eyes, able to switch back in a second.

Take It to the Bank

A FTER WITNESSING THREE DAYS OF Susan's high-class shopping adventure and her coming out to the world of the rich and famous, Isaac watched her prepare for a new day. He found himself speaking to her whenever he forgot his place. And, to his surprise, it seemed as if she heard him.

Mentally tired just trying to keep up with her activity, he would look at her and say, "Rest now. You must be exhausted."

In return, Susan would yawn, put her book down and prepare herself for bed. The more it happened, the more in sync they became.

On another occasion, Isaac gave her specific fashion advice with a little chuckle. "Not *those* shoes!"

As if in reply, Susan said, "Okay. I'll change."

These interactions gave him an incredible sense of purpose, which helped him forget all other distractions. He was in the land of the living by proxy, and it suited him fine. He felt like he had an exclusive front row — an all-expenses-paid ticket to the Susan Mitchell Show — and there was no place he would rather be.

* * *

He basked in its intimacy for three days before it all came crashing down.

"Enough!" Susan exclaimed suddenly to her kitchen as she prepared her breakfast. "Surely this is enough. I already have everything I need."

Isaac looked around the room in complete surprise, expecting to find an unknown companion who may have slipped through the door while his attention was diverted. The room was empty.

He wondered if it was possible that he had inadvertently asked her a question without saying it aloud. However, at that moment, his mind had been clear. Also, he had never done it previously and didn't believe he could. So far, words were still required in this realm.

Susan's outburst had not been an idle afterthought such as "stupid door" or "I would forget my head if it wasn't screwed on," as if she'd left the house without keys. She was talking to somebody the way she had been talking to Isaac. Even if she didn't know it, she was answering a question that had been placed in her head.

Isaac had never considered that he might not be Susan's sole companion. He allowed his vision to stray from her to the space around her. Without a physical body or Susan as a focal point, his vision swung like a gyroscope, moving too fast to pick out anything of the everyday items. He swung his vision around once again but still found nothing.

* * *

"Fella," Isaac called. It had been days since he had used his out-loud voice to the universe, and it croaked and sputtered like a cross between phlegm and static. "Fella! I need to talk to you! Fella, ..."

"Mr. McGlynn, I am here," he cut in, not waiting for Isaac to finish his last summons. "Is everything okay?"

After the passive calm of his new role over the past few days, Isaac was surprised how quickly he had panicked. Just hearing Fella's familiar voice again gave Isaac a sense of comfort. He was the only person he could confide in since his death. For a moment, he'd imagined that, if Fella had not come, he'd drift through the world of the living like a plastic bag on the breeze.

"Thank you for coming," Isaac started before he knew exactly what he would say next.

"Of course, Mr. McGlynn. You are never alone here."

"But I only know you. Who would I call if you did not come?"

"While you are here, I am here. It is that simple. Maybe someday you will be in my space for another soul."

"Please call me Isaac. I don't understand why you keep calling me Mr. McGlynn."

"Because you are a man who pursued power. I want you to feel like you are still empowered here."

"I don't think it is helping me adjust to the new existence. I have no power here. I accept that. I am going to need a friend more now, Fella. Please call me Isaac."

"Okay, Isaac. I am honored to be your friend. I know how exclusive that title has been over the years of your life." Fella paused and then continued. "You called on me, friend? You sounded upset."

Isaac flashed a moment of shame. "I'm sorry. I was caught by surprise, and it scared me. Am I the only soul witnessing Susan's life? I heard her talking to someone else."

"I can tell you only so much on this topic, Isaac," Fella answered calmly. "I can tell you that it is possible for multiple souls to be witnessing a life, just like it can be possible that no one is watching. What I cannot tell you is who it might be or why. You bring your perspective to Susan's life. Perhaps yours is the one she needs for what's to come next. Some other soul may bring their perspective also. The Many Many deemed that it was better for the living to have separation on this plane."

"Why, Fella? I don't understand."

"So you don't become distracted. So you can give them your full attention. Don't let this awareness distract you, Isaac. You have an important job to do, and the next hand of cards is about to be played. You will need to be focused for this."

"Okay. I understand now."

* * *

Isaac returned to Susan's reality. Time had shifted since he'd left. She was wearing the same clothes, so perhaps it was only an hour or two later. He found her pulling another of his former cars into a car park where there was no valet. Once parked, her car stood out like a horse at a pony show. The golden shine of the designer shops from days earlier was now replaced with a blue-gray color scheme. Unlike the other mall, Susan had to negotiate its well-worn paths with schoolchildren, housewives and old men with shopping carts while walking through this one.

She walked into a small bank called TNP Bank, which lined the outside of the complex.

In the bank, Susan approached the first employee she found: a short woman with brown, curly hair in a style that Isaac remembered from old TV shows. He wondered if that branch had been her one and only job throughout her lifetime.

In a quiet but firm manner, Susan asked the clerk, "Can you please tell Paul Derick that Susan Mitchell is here to see him?"

"Yes, ma'am. Is he expecting you?"

"No. I don't have an appointment."

"It may be difficult. Usually you need to schedule a meeting with the branch manager before you come in."

Susan could see that the woman was reluctant to face the wrath of the man in question without at least a scheduled meeting to fall back on.

Susan gently took the clerk's hand and spoke quietly to her. "Tell him that it is Susan Mitchell. He will see me. And if he doesn't, you can tell him that I'll make a scene."

The clerk bit her lip and uttered "oh" under her breath before rushing off to tell an already intimidating man that he had been summoned by a lowly customer.

Isaac braced himself. The drama of Susan's life gripped him more by the minute, and no detail was too small.

Susan did not move. She did not move to one of the available waiting areas or fade into one of the walls as she had done so cleverly as a child. She stood her ground firmly and waited.

It took seven minutes for the man to arrive. He was smaller than Isaac had been expecting him to be, given the fear he had elicited in his employee, but he walked tall to compensate. His thinning gray-black hair was slicked back over his scalp like pavement on a runway. How amazing that hair must have been in its day! Isaac found him striking and wondered if women felt the same. Perhaps they saw him for what he once was and filled in the faded blanks for themselves, maybe with better versions than reality served up. He looked like a man who could treat a woman like a queen until she was his, at which point the relationship would be cruelly re-evaluated in his favor.

Paul Derick approached Susan and, loud enough for others to hear, he spat, "If you think this is how you get my attention, Miss Mitchell, I can assure you that you are mistaken." He had come out fighting and was trying to add public embarrassment to his arsenal of weapons.

"And yet here you are, Paul. Shall we talk out here with all these lovely people? You seem to want to include them in our chat. I could tell them how you help young women who can't afford loans to get them."

If he was angry before, Isaac needed to find a new adjective for the branch manager now.

"How *dare* you!" he said, taking her by the elbow and guiding her toward his office. "I will not have you say such untrue things in front of our customers. Whatever your grievance is, I will hear it in private where you can't poison the minds of others."

Susan smiled and allowed herself to be escorted to the area in which she had wanted to go. Once they were safely in his office, and a small privacy shade was pulled over the only window not made of frosted glass, the man rounded on her instantly.

"What was *that* about?" Paul demanded, insisting that Susan sit down.

"I wanted to see you, Paul. It's been such a long time. Is this the original desk?" Susan ran her hand across it lacquered surface. "It seems so much smaller with my clothes on."

"We had a deal. I helped you when nobody else would. Remember? You had nothing when you came to me."

Susan wasn't finished toying with him. "Do you ever think about that day, or is it a common thing for you? I used to think about it all the time. Then again, some things a girl just needs to do to survive in this world. If I recall rightly, I think … hmm … oh, that's right. You made me kneel there," she said, pointing to a spot directly in front of his office chair. "And there was that second time where you had me bend over this desk."

"How *dare* you! How many people said no to you before I felt sorry for you? How many others wouldn't give you the time of day? I risked a lot to help you buy that apartment of yours. We can't just be doing favors for *anyone* who comes through that door in a short skirt."

Susan didn't allow a single word to break her focus. "You're right, of course. I only have myself to blame. Who did I think I was by being broke and desperate? And coming in here and wasting your valuable time!"

Paul rolled his eyes and was about to protest when Susan let him know that she was not quite finished, whispering, "Although, the more I think about it, it must have given you an incredible sense of power. Do you ever sit in here with your important businesspeople and think about what you got me to do for that loan? Do you ever imagine me back in here, kneeling at your desk, with that power flowing through your veins? I bet you do."

The branch manager feigned disgust, but it was unclear if it was directed at Susan or himself. A vein in his temple became more visible than it had been only a minute ago.

"I hardly even remember who you are. Just another slut, walking in here and looking for money that they don't deserve. You think you're special? You are *nothing*. You are not the first or the last woman who has had to pay my personal fee for service. You should thank me for letting you suck my ..."

"Now, Paul. Let's calm down a little. You are starting to make me afraid for my safety."

Isaac had no doubt that Susan was in complete control of this situation.

"I think it's best that I leave before you hurt me or get any further ideas." She reached into her purse and pulled out a cell phone, pressing something on the screen. "Three, two, one ... and we are done."

"What the hell is going on?" Paul demanded.

"You really were amazing! Thank you. This little session could not have gone better," Susan said, allowing his confusion to linger just a touch longer. "You see, I'm a different person now, Paul. I know a thing or two about power myself. You could say that I've learned from the best!"

Isaac had the distinct impression that she had been casting this last line past Paul and right to him. He could feel the ripples in his water as the compliment founds its mark.

Paul exploded. "What are you *talking* about, you crazy woman!"

"Well, the one thing that I have learned about power since we last met is that power shifts. One moment, you think you have all of it. And then some crazy bitch comes into your office with a cell phone to record your conversation. Then, within moments, your power has betrayed you. You see, power always picks the strongest, and that is no longer you."

The bank manager, unaccustomed to being challenged directly, stood for a moment and seemed to be considering the best direction to lash out. He eyed Susan and then the phone, as if trying to decide which one he should destroy.

Susan, who had left the phone in plain sight and within his reach, simply smiled, daring him to strike out. "Just imagine what that poor wife of yours would say if she ever heard that confession. Or if, by any crazy chance, it was sent to the press with your details. The bank would have to fire you immediately. They would go to so much effort to try and prove to the world that it was all you and not them. I feel for your children. Three now, isn't it?"

"*Nobody* threatens me," Paul said, snatching the phone and grasping it like a snake with a mouse. A cruel smile spread across his face.

Susan did not challenge him. "Smash it," she winked with an encouraging nod. "It will make you feel better. Just know that the recording is not sitting there. It is already safely online. It will be automatically released to the world in two hours if I don't stop it."

The cornered animal suddenly realized that it had underestimated its attacker and placed the phone back on the table. "What do you want? More money?"

"Oh, no," Susan said. "I have plenty of money now. I could buy twenty of those apartments if I wanted to. No, I'm a businesswoman now. I want to own you, as a customer, the same way that you owned me. Don't worry. Nothing messy. Nothing painful — unless of course you don't follow through.

"You see, I have strong friends now also. You are going to be my first customer! Then, you are going to bring me many more. Start saving, Paul, because you're going to need $50,000 to open your account. You should be excited. Our returns are amazing! I will send the banking details and, if that's a problem, I can send someone in a few weeks to collect in person."

Paul covered his mouth as if he was physically keeping his anger at bay.

"Try to remember the good times, Paul. It'll make you feel better." She collected her phone, shook Paul's hand with another smile and left the room.

The Transition

——•——

IN THE DAYS FOLLOWING HER visit to the bank, Susan was enjoying her new money in a way that Isaac never had. For him, money had always been about power and control. An expensive car would be bought or leased because it signaled his success and gave his customers an anchor for their aspirations. If the car didn't work, there was always a boat, a plane, women or simple intimidation.

Isaac had been told by an early mentor, "Money attracts money. Show them what they want, and then tell them that working with you is the only way they will get it." It had been a very profitable business model.

Susan, on the other hand, respected money in a completely different way. Perhaps it was because she had not created the vast majority of it herself. The power it brought her was not treated as a birthright but instead a luxury to be enjoyed. She would buy the most expensive item on the menu, and then eat every mouthful as if it could be her last. She didn't seem to be mourning Isaac's passing, which he was happy about, but which still hurt him slightly. He wondered if it was because she was still talking to him daily.

* * *

Isaac was enjoying another morning in Susan's life when her phone rang.

"Hello?" she answered in a hollow tone without checking the caller ID.

Isaac hoped that it might be one of her friends. He was yet to see her take a single call from a friendly or loving voice and dearly wanted it for her.

The man's voice cracked like a whip. "I hope you have my money, bitch."

The threat landed its blow on Susan's face before she found a little of her magic once again.

Isaac thought that her expression was like a lit bulb being smashed into a hundred pieces and reassembling itself instantly with a small crack, which had not been there before. "The living don't see the cracks," he thought.

Susan took a breath and calmly addressed the caller through a bitter smile. "So, you think that it is in your interest to keep trying to intimidate me? You don't understand. I could quite happily have had you killed already if I'd wanted to. I am a rich woman now, remember? And rich, powerful women want what rich, powerful women want. So, right now, the only reason you still have breath to spit those angry words is because I allow you to breathe."

"You don't scare me."

"Which tells me that you are not very smart. You don't think I know who you are, but I know everything about you. You see, I know how to hide, I'm so good at it in fact that it was the only thing that kept me alive as a child. I have been watching you. And I can tell you now that tiny little gun of yours is not going to get you a cent more than I have already agreed to pay. For your own safety, I suggest that you don't bring it." Then, she added with a laugh to prove that she was truly amused, "Now where and when should we meet?"

Isaac had to wonder how much of Susan's behavior had been his influence and how much was her own. She had copied his intimidation technique perfectly. The anger behind it was what really made it work, and he had not taught her that. It was perhaps the legacy they both took from their abusive childhood.

When the man finally found his voice, it had lost all its former venom. He was now a child forced to say that he was sorry for something he was not sorry about. His words dripped with disgust. "So, tell me then, how *you* want to do this?"

"Let's keep it an easy swap. We'll meet tomorrow afternoon at two. The same coffee shop we met at last time. We'll swap money for photos and go our separate ways, never to cross paths again."

"Done," he said and hung up.

Susan looked at her phone and seemed to be replaying parts of the conversation in her mind. The smiling and giggling she had used as a prop had disappeared from her face the moment the call was over. To Isaac, she did not seem completely unhappy with her role play.

Isaac was fully aware of the strategy and knew that a lot of it had been a complete bluff. Now, with the acid smell of the call still in her nostrils, Susan looked for a more pleasant distraction.

Isaac brought himself closer to give her some comfort. He had been hovering at a steady distance of about 3 feet over the past few days, which gave him a great vantage point of her face. Now, coming closer, he could pick up her scent and something a bit more: her essence. At that moment, her essence was stained with fear.

Isaac took in a deep breath of her and whispered, "Call John!"

Susan looked across to her left, toward Isaac, like a voice was calling her off in the distance. She rubbed her neck and creased her brow before straightening her head once again. This time, she rotated it in the opposite direction. Regardless of whether another witness was giving her council or Susan was weighing her options, it made little difference to Isaac. He wanted her safe and that was what John could offer her.

Isaac leaned forward once again and whispered, "Call John. Whatever it is, he can help you." He took leave of her personal space and retreated to the standard safety zone.

Susan allowed the second voice one last pitch before tilting her head back in Isaac's direction. This time, she followed it with the rest of her body to face the window to her right. She selected a number from her cell phone and waited for it to ring.

"John, it's Susan. I really need your help!"

Isaac felt a pang of guilt at the first mortal mention of his friend's name. He had been so immersed in the beauty of Susan Mitchell and her real life that he had forgotten to check on his oldest and only friend.

* * *

"Fella, I need to talk to you," Isaac said into the ether.

Although he had no expectation of seeing his heavenly friend, Isaac looked around the room anyway. When the voice finally responded, it was not from within the room or even from within Isaac's head as before. This time, the voice of Fella approached from afar and seemed to be walking step by step toward Isaac at its own pace.

"Hello, Mr. McGlynn … I'm sorry. I mean Isaac. We are friends now after all," Fella said quite sincerely. "I was hoping that you might call on me soon. Please give me a little time to get to you."

Isaac waited a moment for him to approach.

"Now, Isaac," he said in a warm, friendly tone. "What exactly can I do for you? Have you forgotten something or perhaps someone?"

"Yes, Fella. I need to check on John. It has been selfish of me to stay with Susan for so long."

"Ahh. As they say, music to my ears. It seems that John has been wilting without the sunshine of his oldest and dearest friend. He needs your witness."

"Why didn't you tell me this earlier? I would have gone to him already. He is my responsibility, after all," Isaac said, allowing a little of his guilt to pass through his words.

"I am sorry, Isaac. I cannot tell you to do anything. I can help you interpret what you see but cannot be another set of eyes for you."

"You *knew* that he needed me, and you said nothing!"

"There is so much I know that I cannot tell you unless you ask. As I explained to you once before, I have many answers without questions. Would you like to go to him now, Isaac? I can take you there right away. I think it would be best."

"Yes, please. Take me to him. Susan will be okay for now. She's stronger than I thought she was."

* * *

The world of Susan Mitchell unfocused and dissolved. A new, darker world presented itself to Isaac, and the first thing he saw were drawn curtains. A few thin blades of light gave Isaac perspective on where he was and what was in front of him.

A broken version of John Hannebery sat in the dark at the kitchen table. He had just heard those magic words from Susan — "John, I really need your help" — and he now searched the table wildly as if the answers were sketched into its surface.

It was clear that the room was the product of an interior designer's wet dream. Now, each item of expensive furniture had been molested in some way. A white leather couch, designed and made in Paris, had an almost empty beer bottle in its creases and pizza stains on its arms. It was easy for Isaac to tell that it was pizza because a once-chewed slice still lay by one of the legs. The $10,000 television, which John had been so proud to tell Isaac about months ago, now hung precariously from its mount, ready to surrender to gravity and throw itself at the mercy of its connected cables at any moment.

The epicenter of this destruction was John. The blast zone started with him and would have continued had the walls not provided a barrier.

The phone in John's hand found its voice. "John, can you hear me? It's Susan. I really need your help. Will you help me?"

Isaac noticed the single most disturbing aspect of the room. It wasn't the empty beer bottles thrown into the corners, the four perfect lines of cocaine on the table with evidence of many already consumed or the dilated pupils that had turned John's eyes into bottomless saucers. It was the gun, comfortably sitting as a counterweight in John's right hand.

"Me?" he asked, looking wildly around the room and taking in the destruction as if he were afraid that Susan could somehow see it. "Why do you want *my* help?"

Isaac listened to the call as Susan's voice grew soft. "Because I may have some trouble coming, John. And you're the only person still alive whom I trust."

"*Me?*" It was the only response that John could bring himself to say.

"Yes, John. *You.* You and Isaac mean more to me than you know. Will you help me?"

John blinked and looked around in drugged bewilderment. He even pointed to the room and then back at his chest, having a silent, internal conversation. Finally, he looked down at the phone to ensure that he wasn't hallucinating.

Isaac leaned forward and whispered in John's ear for the first time. "She needs you."

Finally satisfied that Susan and her request were real, John blinked. This time, when his eyes opened, the pupils were smaller and more focused. Another person may not have noticed, but Isaac saw it.

As a single, solitary tear caressed John's nose on its journey south, he cleared his throat. "Of course, I'll help you." He clicked open the chamber on the gun with his other hand, letting a single bullet fall silently to the carpet. "Umm ... I'll come to you. I just need to get a little cleaned up first."

The Tipping Point

———•———

ISAAC WATCHED AS JOHN FUMBLED when getting the essential information for his meeting with Susan the following day. Once he had the place and time confirmed, John terminated the call as fast as common decency would allow. He didn't close the call with a light tap-tap of his thumb but instead punched the screen wildly with both thumbs like it was alive.

He looked down to the ground where his gun and its ejected bullet lay and wildly kicked each of them to different parts of the room before he burst into tears. When John's tears fell, they fell hard. To Isaac, who watched in despair, John's face read exasperation, exhaustion and relief. This emotional storm lasted about two and half minutes, but it was the longest two and a half minutes of Isaac McGlynn's death.

Finally, as the sobs subsided, John Hannebery pulled himself together. He ran his hand across his face and used his damp palm to mop the powder from the table, crossing the room to empty the lot into the sink. He turned on the faucet to wash away the remains, and then applied the water vigorously to his face, as if doing so would also cleanse his bloodstream.

Then he made a phone call. "Hey, it's me. John Hannebery. I need you to come back and clean for me."

Isaac sensed a defiant stand on the other end of the line.

John pinched the top of his nose and closed his eyes. "I
know what I said, and I'm sorry. I'm going through some
stuff at the moment with my friend dying, and I really didn't
mean it. Can you please come back? I need you to work for
me again and help me clean up this place." He opened his
eyes and waited for an answer. A moment later, he got it.
"Thank you. I really appreciate it. I'll make it up to you."

Isaac viewed John's face and searched his eyes. The call
from Susan had not given him a new life, only a stay of exe-
cution. Isaac wondered if helping Susan this one time would
be enough to save John from picking up that gun again and
holding it to his head.

* * *

"Fella!"

"Yes, Isaac," he replied almost immediately. "I am still
here with you."

"What exactly happened here? What would have happened if Susan hadn't called or I didn't tell her to? Would
John be dead?"

Fella took a moment to consider his response. "We can
only be sure of what is happening, Isaac, because we see it.
What could have been will always be a mystery. The only
way that we will know what is to come is because we will
witness it. You will see that reality has a way of sharpening
the focus of possibility. You whispered, she called, and the
arm with the gun fell. That is what happened."

"But why is he like this, Fella? What's wrong with him?"

"We see, but we don't always understand, Isaac. You will have to figure it out for yourself. We can never know what is happening in their heads. Let me caution you. You may have played a small part in keeping John Hannebery alive on this occasion. However, his life, and that of Susan's, is not yours to control. You are their witness, Isaac, and perhaps from time to time you may be able to whisper a small suggestion in their ears. That is all. You are not their god."

"And what of him, Fella? Where was God when John put that gun to his temple?" Isaac asked like an angry child.

"I cannot say, Isaac. If God exists, he or she has not been made known to the Many Many. I'm sorry if I disappoint you. I know that others are unhappy to hear this news. It is usually because they expect God to be just like them. Perhaps the Many Many serve the purpose of God. If we do, then we do so through humble witness alone."

"Great! So God is a committee. I didn't need him in life, so there's no point needing him in death. Thank you, Fella. I will return to John now."

* * *

Isaac had always made sure that John had been taken care of. When it got difficult for Isaac to bring women back to their apartment because of John's presence, he had rented another apartment for John close by and had a designer furnish it.

When they made their fortune, Isaac ensured that, regardless of what happened to him and the business, John would never have to work again if he chose not to. His finances had been secured for life, and all John knew was that Isaac had taken care of it. John had never asked about the details. He had simply trusted his orphan brother and nodded.

As they walked through the house that Isaac had purchased for him, Isaac noticed something he had never considered before. Each of the beautiful items of furniture stood to full attention. Outside the room of destruction that they had just left, with its virgin bullets on the floor, the rest of the house was impeccably clean. It was so clean that it indicated no personal taste. In fact, nothing looked like it had ever been used.

It could have been owned by a rich executive as a home away from home or a fully furnished rental property, ready at any moment for the right kind of money to walk through the front door. The one person who did not fit the bill as a tenant, outside of the room of destruction, was John. The art hanging from the walls displayed no identity, and no photographs stood as preserved memories for the casual viewer. What Isaac had once considered a sleek and stylish bachelor pad, it now had the feel of a serviced apartment, built for the rich for short-term living and able to be left behind at a minute's notice.

Isaac, desperate to talk to his old friend, leaned in close and whispered into his ear, "What happened to you, John?"

But, unlike Susan, John gave no indication of having heard Isaac's words. He simply carried out his walk of misery to the shower where he held his head under the running water like a man trying to wash away his shame.

John showered until the skin on his fingers pruned, his face flushed, and the heat threatened to buckle his knees. He used what little energy had not been stolen by the steam to dry himself and find his way to bed where he slept naked for ninety-three minutes.

Isaac watched the entire time, whispering words like a mantra and watching the sleeping man for signs of recognition. "It's Isaac. I'm back, friend. I am with you now. I will protect you."

After many repetitions, John's sleeping posture changed. It was minute but positive. He stopped his violent spasms and removed his face from the pillow, allowing it to face the world for the first time. His soul was still not whole, but it was now one step less short of being completely broken. Isaac allowed himself a moment of silent celebration.

* * *

"Fella, are you there?" Isaac found himself asking before he had even considered why.

"Yes, Isaac. I am always here."

"It's not enough. This whispering. It's not enough."

"It is the tool we have at our disposal, Isaac. I would say that you have used it quite well on this occasion. John is sleeping soundly."

"My only friend nearly put a gun to his head and pulled the trigger, and the best I can do is whisper to him that everything is going to be okay? It's not *enough*!"

"But, Isaac, whispering is the tool ..."

"... at our disposal. Yes, you've told me that already. He is a broken man. His life is draining out of him. I need to have a proper conversation with him. Can you make it happen, Fella? I have money."

Fella's response was not immediate, which made Isaac

wonder if he was already asking the Many Many or if he was just questioning why he had been given such a difficult charge.

Finally, Fella's voice returned with a sad flavor. "What you have requested is possible. We can slip you into John's dream. This is only granted in extreme cases and comes at a heavy price. It is agreed that this case is significant because it will help you understand and not simply be a voyeur. However, the price being paid makes me sad."

"It is only money. That's part of the reason I brought it with me. I will happily pay it. How much do you want?"

"Some. Measurement doesn't matter here, but we will relieve you of some of it. That is not what makes me sad. The price you will pay is insignificant on this occasion. The price that the soul at the other end of this transaction may pay could be great. Your money may not help them the way they think, but they are willing to take your bargain."

"Can you tell me more, Fella?"

"No, Isaac. Your side of the transaction ends with me. I broker this transaction on your behalf. The seller will remain anonymous until — and only if — they wish not to be."

"Tell me again why I exist in this form?"

"To witness the living, to give them validation and for them to do the same to you."

"Then I have no choice. I need to keep my friend alive as long as I can. I do this by prolonging his life in any way possible. The cost borne by me or others in this existence is irrelevant," Isaac said, finding more confidence in every word. "Please put me on a stage with John."

Fella sighed, and it occurred to Isaac that, for a being who didn't need to breathe, the gesture was likely for his benefit.

* * *

Isaac's world dissolved and rearranged itself into a reality similar to his rewinds.

He heard the last of Fella's voice in his head, which sounded like he was reading from a script. "Your time with John will be short. While there, you must acknowledge your passing, or it could cause him great confusion and more emotional pain when he wakes. Finally, you need to keep the message simple. When he wakes, he may forget things you discussed, become disorientated or even ignore the dream altogether. Keep it simple, deliver your message and terminate the connection."

"You make it sound like a phone call, Fella."

"In a way, it is, Isaac. A phone call from heaven."

The Phone Call
from Heaven

———•———

"JOHN. IT'S ME ... ISAAC."

Isaac had been dropped into John's dream of the moment. There had been no fancy introduction or parting of the clouds. Only a small boy — Isaac in child form, who was not there one moment and then, in the flutter of an eye, was. Taking his child form was not completely alien to Isaac after having spent time viewing himself as such during his recent rewinds. It soon made sense as he looked around the room. He was back in the place that had haunted them both: the orphanage.

"Oh, god. Not *here* again!" Isaac said to himself in a child's body but with a man's voice.

Sitting on the bed across from him, right where he had always been, was John Junior: the same child who had beaten three larger boys on Isaac Junior's beckoning all those years ago. However, this dreaming view of John was before the bully bashing. The two boys knew of each other at this point but had not yet formed their alliance.

"John, it's me," Isaac said, trying to catch the boy's eye.

John adjusted his gaze. When he spoke, it was with the voice of the adult that he would become. "Isaac, is that really *you*? What are you doing here?"

"It's me, old friend. We need to talk, and we don't have much time."

"You shouldn't be here, Isaac."

"Why, John? Why are you here? This is your dream after all."

"You left me, and this is the place without you, Isaac. It was me before you, and it has now become me without you. I come back here every time I sleep, and I wait."

"You wait for what, John?"

"For Brother Anthony to come."

Isaac's fear was immediate but undefined. There was something about the look in John's eyes that put Isaac's soul on ice. Fear and resignation. The devil, who was about to enter this dream, would damage John in a way that he had before and would likely do again.

John interrupted Isaac's confusion. "You know what the worst is, Isaac? In the morning, I never remember what I'm scared of."

"Stop, John!" Isaac screamed. "Stop this dream now! It's in your head."

The air in the room changed. It became cold and hollow.

"It's too late, Isaac."

Isaac felt the change before he had even realized that they were no longer alone. The hollow echo of Brother Anthony, which had haunted their childhood, burst into the room out of nowhere. Without warning or hesitation, he viciously slapped John across the face.

"Stop!" Isaac screamed at the ghost, but he didn't listen.

Brother Anthony continued the physical onslaught until the child's cheeks started to redden and swell.

Isaac tried to come to his friend's aid, but it was no use.

Then Isaac cried "Stop!" again.

This time, the ghost of Brother Anthony heard him. He turned and grinned at Isaac as he raised his hand to John once again. He let his blow find its mark and, as it did, Isaac heard his menacing voice. *"You cannot stop me here."*

* * *

"Fella!" Isaac yelled. "I need you!"

Isaac heard a response, but it was from a distant location. "I cannot help you there, Isaac. You are in another man's dream. I cannot see what you see. It is a fiction created in John's head."

Knowing that Fella was not going to be any help, Isaac had no alternative but to ignore him completely and find his own solution to the situation.

* * *

Isaac tried to throw himself at Brother Anthony and come to his friend's aid, but John was still glued to his spot, battered and broken. Isaac screamed at Brother Anthony again to try and redirect some of the aggression onto himself, but it didn't work.

Isaac tried a different strategy. "John, look at me!"

The child's head jerked up as if he had forgotten that Isaac was in the room. Their eyes found each other and held.

"John, I'm here with you. I'm sorry I left you, but I'm back now. Send him away."

Brother Anthony threw another grimacing smile in Isaac's direction, but this time there was a shift in John's face.

"John? You are not alone anymore. I'm back now."

"He will only be back tomorrow, Isaac."

"Then I will be with you, and we will face him together. Today, tomorrow and forever!"

As Brother Anthony's fist landed on John's face this time, it did not penetrate the skin. The child had turned into stone and Brother Anthony's fist shattered into pieces like crystal falling on a cement floor. The shatter ran up the ghost's arm and into the rest of his body. The sinister smile dissolved into nothing as the shatter worked its way through his face. Within a moment, all the shattered shards of the devil had become dust in the lamp light.

"Sleep now, John," Isaac pleaded. "This nightmare is over. And, this time, if nothing else, remember that I am back with you again."

John blinked and nodded once, and the dream faded. Isaac once again viewed John as a sleeping adult.

* * *

"Fella? Are you with me?"

"Yes, Isaac. How can I assist you?"

"You can start by telling me what the hell *that* was all about!" Isaac screamed. "Why in God's name was Brother Anthony in John's dream? Did he not do enough damage to us while he was still alive? Is he haunting John? Do I need to kill his ghost also?"

The air in the room went bitterly cold in an instant. John turned in his sleep and pulled the blanket up to his chin.

Although Isaac did not have physical form, he could feel John's discomfort at the extremities of his soul.

Now Fella's voice was amplified in volume and anger. "Isaac, I am here to guide you, so let me give you this warning once only. Taking a life is the highest sin. The Many Many forgave you the first time as you were young and under duress, but you should not push your luck. Do not threaten to take a life or a death in this existence or you can say goodbye to your friends — and perhaps even to yourself — forever. They may not be able to discipline the living, but I assure you that they can the dead. Do you understand?"

"Yes, I understand. It won't happen again, but please tell me why Brother Anthony is haunting John's dreams."

"Whomever or whatever you saw was not Brother Anthony. He has moved on," Fella said in calmer tone. "There is no place for the likes of him as a witness. He was denied entry to this plane and is already back with a new life and a new timeline. He's teaching himself the art of inflicting misery once again."

"Already back with a new life? Like reincarnation?"

"Isaac, you talk about it like he was given a prize. He is so far from his destination that a step backward may even be a step forward. You, Isaac, are a witness. You are one step closer every day."

"And what is my destination?"

"That is not a conversation for today. You will need more context first. It's best if I explain that at the right time."

Isaac wasn't happy with the answer. He didn't want another explanation full of riddles that he didn't understand, so he asked another question. "Why do we have people like him, Fella?"

"Because a great wrong was done to him many lifetimes ago, and he is still angry. He doesn't even know why anymore, and we can't reach him. He is like a wildfire that consumes all in its path. They cannot be stopped, but eventually they run out of fuel or burn themselves out."

"Then why is John still dreaming of him?"

"Because he misses you, Isaac, and it's his mind's way of telling him so. He saved you from the world, and you saved him from his own fears. You got your closure from Brother Anthony, but you were the lucky one. Many didn't see the broken man you left dead on that floor. They still see the tormentor in their dreams."

"Then what can I do for him?"

"Just be his friend and his life witness. I remind you that it is the highest of honors. Make sure his life is validated."

"And what about Susan?"

"You have them both to watch over. She is stronger than you think. Also, she has witness from another. Her life will be validated without you watching over her every step."

* * *

At that moment, John let out a deep breath and shifted in his sleep again. He was starting to wake up, so Isaac resumed his vigil.

John stretched his limbs and raked his fingers through his hair. He swung his legs around the side of the bed and tried to sit up in a slow, labored effort. Due to the excessive drugs in his system when he went to sleep, he did not end in a final seated position. Instead, it was approximately where he thought his body should be.

Even though it had been many years since Isaac had taken drugs, he recalled the feeling. After making their first million dollars, the brothers had celebrated with a three-day binge of drugs and the finest women that money could buy. When they both had finally slept, Isaac wondered if he would ever wake up again. Eighteen hours later, when their eyes had opened, they had each visibly aged over ten years. Looking at John now as he moved his body from his bed, it seemed as if Isaac had been dead for over fifteen years. In effect, it had only been a matter of days.

As John walked from the bedroom to the bathroom, he rubbed his temple. It was clear that something was out of reach and that he was searching for a thread of it to help him uncover the rest.

Isaac watched him closely for the next twenty minutes, but John showed no visible signs of remembering his dream or Isaac's words. The experience seemed to be lost forever.

That's What
Friends Are For

"JOHN, ARE YOU OKAY? You look like crap," Susan remarked.

Seeing Susan and John together again in the same room gave Isaac an unexpected wave of relief like fitting two pieces of a jigsaw puzzle together. Without him in the middle, there would be no transition color. Perhaps, as the bigger picture evolved, they wouldn't need it. Isaac hoped so, but he wasn't convinced. He thought they would need at least a little finesse from him along the way.

John had made his way over to Susan's apartment an hour after waking and eating a little food. Susan's version of John looking like crap was much better than Isaac's version of John hours before. Both were in stark contrast and a vast improvement on the drug-fueled suicidal John of the previous day.

"Don't worry about me," John growled. "I'm here to help you now. We can worry about me later."

"Okay ..." Susan sighed.

John picked up on her hesitation and said, "Don't worry, I'll be fine."

"Okay. When this is over, we will fix whatever is wrong with you. We should look after each other now," Susan said with a reassuring pat on his forearm.

John looked confused. "I never got what was between you two," he admitted. "You are beautiful, without a doubt, and he was a rich man, but there seemed to be something I was missing."

"He didn't know what it was either," Susan said, a little disappointed. "And I really should have told him before he died. Anyway, that's a story for another day. We don't have much time before our little meeting."

"Right! Let's get down to business. Who is this guy, and what does he want?"

"Let me tell you just enough to deal with the situation at hand. I don't want to get caught in the back story right now. I promise to tell you everything else later. Honestly, I'm tired of secrets," Susan said, looking for agreement before proceeding.

Both John and Isaac leaned in, eager for details. John gave her a nod and a wave to continue.

"I am very good at hiding," Susan began. "You could say that, for many years, my life depended on it. One day, way before I ever walked into your office, I was watching over it. Don't panic! I don't work for the police or anything. We can discuss the reasons later. Anyway, I'd been camping out at Marco's Cafe, across the street from the office, the first day as a blonde, then a redhead, a few days later a brunette — different orders every time. Not even the staff knew that I was the same person. As I sat there watching, I noticed that I was not the only one doing so.

"I was getting a little bored of watching the office, so I started to stake out this new guy instead. He followed you when you did your rounds with the investors, and I followed him. He followed Isaac as he met with company directors and high-class hookers, and again I followed him. He took photos of everything you both did."

Susan then switched from memory to analytics. "Now, John, at this point I had two options. I could have approached you both and warned you, but neither of you knew me at all. How would it have looked? No, that would have ruined everything that I had worked for."

"And what *exactly* had you been working for?" John asked, looking a little betrayed.

"No, wait! That's not what I meant. It was not about money, if that's what you think. You could take every cent right now if I could get Isaac back. It was always just about getting close to you and Isaac, nothing more. Again, I will explain better later when there's more time. Okay?"

"Continue," John said skeptically.

"Okay. Option one was out of the question, so I had option two. One day, I followed this guy back to a small office on the other side of town and found out that he was a private investigator. Figuring that he was unlikely to be a killer, I approached him and asked him outright why he was following you both."

"And?" John asked.

"He said that he had been collecting information on you both for a disgruntled client."

"Who?" John demanded.

Susan put up both hands defensively. "I don't know. No matter how hard I pushed, he wouldn't tell me."

"I could make him talk," John declared proudly.

"Yes, I'm sure you could. You were never supposed to know. He showed me some of the material he had, and it was very damning to both of you. Of course, I had been watching over you for some time, but I wasn't collecting information to bring you down. He was. There was enough there to put you both behind bars for years, and I could never have that. I told him that I would pay him above whatever his client was paying for the material."

"And how much was that?"

"Two hundred and fifty thousand dollars," Susan answered through a frown. "The only problem was that I was almost broke."

"Why would you *pay* that, Susan? If you cared so much, why wouldn't you just approach us about it? We had plenty of money."

"Because it was my job to look after you boys. I had done it before, and I would do it again. I honestly thought about approaching you. I dressed myself up the way Isaac liked his women to look, walked right into that office of yours and waited. The moment I saw Isaac face to face, after all those years, I froze. I knew he hated his assistant, so I just made up a new strategy on the spot and said that I was there to replace her. I got the job."

John sighed. "This story is crazy. As you said, let's fill in the blanks later. The money ... where did you get the money to pay him? We didn't pay you *that* much."

"I got him to give me a few months to sort out the finances. I think he thought that I was going to steal it from the company. I could *never* do that to you guys. I was running out of time, so I got a loan. It was the sort of loan where I had to suck a bank manager's cock to get it approved, but I got it. Two hundred and fifty thousand was sitting in my account. I was ready to pay him, but Isaac got sick and everything turned to shit." The emotion of Isaac's illness stole a moment from her.

Isaac, who had been watching the entire discussion from John's side, felt the breath she took. The sorrow that traveled down her spine went down his own. It was the first time that he had seen her show any emotion over his death. He took a moment to savor the connection he had with her.

Susan regained her composure. "You remember how busy I was preparing everything for Isaac? I hardly left the office for days. I missed the deadline to pay him, and he started to think that he wasn't going to get his money. He got aggressive with me and doubled the price."

"Has he touched you?" John said through gritted teeth.

"No, but he's aggressive, and I can't keep bluffing him. If I threaten him again, I need to be able to come through or I'm toast."

"I don't fully trust you yet, but I won't let that happen."

"Thank you. That's what I was hoping. Let me tell you what I want to do. I still want to pay him. I don't want Isaac's name dragged through the mud now that he's dead, and I don't want you going to jail. So, basically, I want to do the deal. I was hoping that you could wait in the shadows to make sure I don't get killed. Do you think you can do that?"

"I will keep you safe, Susan."

Isaac could see the wave of relief wash over Susan's face as she heard John's words. He studied John's face to try and see if it had merely been out of duty to him, pity for Susan or simply to get access to a man who had been plotting against him. He wasn't sure that even he knew the answer.

John spoke again as if an afterthought had caught him

by the collar. "Wait! You mentioned that you had helped us before. What's *that* all about?"

"I'll tell you more later. Yes, I've come to your assistance three times over the past few years. I cleaned up for you a few years back, after you left Lance Rampe battered at the top of a flight of stairs. What you don't know is that, after you left, Lance in his dizziness fell down those stairs. If I hadn't removed the CCTV footage and called the ambulance to tell them that he had been drunk and fell, you would be locked up for murder. You of all people should know that a dead body creates a lot of questions."

"You can't be *serious*!" John snapped. "Lance was okay when I left him. Sure, I may have gotten a little carried away, but he was conscious. I've never, *ever* killed anyone!"

"John, you got carried away alright! You are going to have to watch — or at least channel — that temper of yours or it is going to get you into a lot of trouble. Lance was heavily concussed and completely disorientated when you left him, which is when he fell. I called it in and got the footage before anyone saw anything. Also, for the record, I believe you that you haven't killed anyone. You are not that sort of guy."

Susan was getting flustered. She had obviously not planned to go into so much detail with John that quickly. Perhaps she had underestimated him all these years.

Susan tapped her watch. "John, we only have forty-five minutes until my meeting with him. We can go through all this later, and I promise you that I will be completely honest and tell you anything you want to know."

"Okay, but you owe me answers," John replied without hesitating.

John still looked slightly broken and disheveled. However, at his size and strength, he was more like a muscle car with a broken headlight and three different color doors than a collection of damaged parts.

When he spoke now, his voice changed, and he was focused on the task at hand. "Call him. Call him now and tell him that you will come to him. Tell him that you have the money and will come alone. Make sure that he doesn't try anything. If you can, try and sound a little scared."

"I *am* scared!"

"Good. It will help."

Be Careful What You Wish For

B Y THE TIME SUSAN WAS scheduled to arrive at the office of the private investigator, John had already been in the building for over fifteen minutes. Luckily enough, the building housed multiple businesses, so it was easy for him to pretend to be there for someone else.

John decided that it was best not to arrive at the same time as Susan in case the entryway was being watched. Instead, he chose the disguise of a doting boyfriend. He wore all the clothes that John Hannebery would not wear — sneakers, skinny jeans, an oversized T-shirt and a baseball cap coupled with a bunch of flowers and a box of muffins. It had gotten him through the door and up the elevator without any attention, except for a little encouragement by an elderly lady who was cheering on young love.

Isaac had sent John on many questionable errands over the years, but this was the first time he had actually been on one with him. In the past, Isaac would simply have said something like, "We need to convince our favorite customer to up his investment by fifty percent" or "I don't believe that

Sean is telling us everything he knows about the fund." In doing so, Isaac would wind John up, point him in the right direction and let him go. The problem would be solved miraculously.

Sitting (figuratively) alongside John in a restroom, a floor above his target, Isaac was quite surprised as to the extent of John's creativity. Isaac had seen him consider the floor layout of his target and had prepared Susan for their encounter by telling her it was best that she didn't know from where or when he would arrive. John also had told her that he would enter the situation only if needed.

John's watch signaled the turn of the hour and the time for action. He stood up and stretched his body to make sure that he was ready for anything physical. He flushed for no reason other than to avoid suspicion, washed his hands and made his way to the elevator. He no longer had the props he had entered the building with, having given them to a receptionist for a separate business on the floor where he had been hiding in exchange for directions to the restroom. The only thing that he had kept was the baseball cap in case of overhead-surveillance cameras.

John had promised Susan that he would only come in if things got out of hand. Isaac could see from the look on John's face that it was unlikely a promise he would keep.

By the time John burst into the private detective's office, Isaac could see that things had already gotten out of hand. The man was at least a foot taller than John, but he didn't have the body mass to intimidate him. He was a fair-haired rake, who was now standing over Susan as if he intended to strike or at the very least threaten her.

The last word leaving his mouth as the door flung open

— "you ..." — clung to the edges of his mouth like it was scared to jump.

The private detective looked up in surprise. By the time he recognized John, it was too late.

To Isaac, it was obvious that he knew enough about John to be scared.

John didn't even break his stride. He didn't have to. It took him three steps to reach the man and another to ram his head into the side wall. The detective fell to the ground, dazed and holding his nose, which had now started dripping thick drops of rich, red blood onto the carpet.

"John!" Susan said, startled.

Isaac thought that perhaps Susan hadn't needed John's intervention at that particular moment. She certainly hadn't expected it so soon or with such force. He also thought that the guy's face was fucked. It was the first time in death that he had sworn. The word and the sentiment felt dirty, and he instantly regretted it.

The now-bloodied detective moaned and spat blood.

John knelt down beside him. "You've been taking photos of me and Isaac, huh? Where's your camera right now? You could get a real close-up." John grabbed the hair on the back of his head like a passionate lover might do before a kiss, and then slammed the man's face into the side wall once more. This time, the collision left a bloody smudge on the wall on impact.

Isaac looked up at Susan. She was clearly distressed. In all that she had been through in her lifetime, it seemed that physical violence had not played a big part. Seeing John brutalize the man who had threatened her so many times on their calls did not bring her any joy.

"John!" she screamed. "Please stop!"

John didn't hear her. He grabbed the man's head again and prepared to leave another blood stamp on the wall.

"John, no!" Susan screamed again. Her cheeks were wet with tears.

Isaac had seen John's anger before, but it had been many years. However, this was not an honest beating. It was turning into a brutal bashing, and something needed to be done soon.

The detective was on his hands and knees, groaning and dripping his blood onto the floor.

Isaac brought himself close and whispered into John's ear. "John, you are frightening Susan."

As before, John showed no sign of having heard Isaac. He stood up, kicked the detective in the stomach and shouted, "You want to bring me and Isaac down! You threaten to kill Susan!" They weren't questions but simply a list of grievances to justify the punishment. He smiled viciously. "I don't fucking think so."

The detective's body had curled into a protective ball. John lined himself up to kick him in the head. Susan screamed and covered her eyes.

Isaac had no time left for false whispers. He had to shout, and he had to shout loudly. "JOHN, STOP THIS NOW!"

John immediately stopped his leg swing and looked wildly about the room. "Isaac."

Relieved, Isaac reverted back to the whisper. "Susan is scared. Make sure that she's okay."

John looked at Susan, but he was distracted. He was still looking for the Isaac behind the voice in his head. He reached out his hand for Susan, but she backed away. "Are you okay?"

"I'm … I'm fine," she said before finally agreeing to take his hand.

John pulled her around and behind him, and then reached down to pick up the bloodied detective. He lifted the man and slammed him into the empty chair behind the desk. Then he winked at Susan to assure her that he was back in charge of his senses before taking one last quick scan of the room. It was clear to Isaac that John had heard something at that moment, and it had snapped him back from the brink.

John returned his attention to the detective. As he had expected, he found a small gun taped to the underside. He held up the gun for inspection and to let his captor know that he had it. "Makes sense to protect yourself. You never know who could come barging in while you're physically intimidating a woman half your size."

The detective wiped blood from his face and scoffed. "I'm confused. Are you protecting her from me or from yourself?" he said, laughing through the pain in his face. "I just take pictures. I don't hurt people like you do."

John checked the gun to make sure it was loaded. When he realized that it was, he pointed it at the detective. "That's the problem!" he said in a menacing tone. "I don't like people taking pictures of me without my knowledge." He turned the computer screen to face the man. "You are going to delete them all now. Right here in front of me. You either do that and satisfy me that it's done, or I start smashing things. I will start with your stuff and maybe move on to your fingers."

The man reluctantly pivoted the screen so that he and John could see its contents. He grabbed for the mouse and clicked through various directories. "You see this file here? It has your names on it."

John acknowledged the folder but put a hand out to stop the man. He scanned the other names on the list, and one seemed to catch his attention. He quickly pretended that it hadn't.

Isaac tried to peer over John's shoulder to see the list for himself, but the screen showed him nothing but a white glare. No amount of virtual soul blinking brought it into focus.

John raised his hand. "Okay. Delete it and your backup. I'll let you keep everything else."

The man clicked on files and pressed the delete key. He demonstrated to John that he had done the job thoroughly enough that they could not be retrieved later.

Isaac was distracted. He still could not see the computer screen with any clarity and began to realize that anything with a digital screen was beyond his reach. The screen gave him no signal, as if it had no power or was pure, ugly light. It felt like a TV set emitting low-grade radiation.

When the bloodied man finished deleting the files, John stood to leave. He took the bullets out of the gun, put them in one of his pockets and placed the gun on the desk.

The bloodied man, realizing that his life was no longer on the line, allowed himself one outburst. "I'm just trying to make a living, you know?"

"I know. That's why I left your business intact. You were just given the wrong targets at the wrong time. You can thank your client for that!" John said before heading for the door.

Susan seemed a little surprised that things had wrapped up so quickly. She asked John, "Don't you want to know who his client is?"

John smiled as he held open the door for her. "Nah. That's his business."

Susan started to leave but, as she passed the private investigator, she paused and reached into her bag. She pulled out a big bundle of money and put it on the table in front of him.

"As you can probably tell, I don't have any control over John. Also, if you had given me the chance, I would have given you the money without any of this trouble. After all, it's not like I don't have it now. The problem was that you were starting to scare me, and I needed to protect myself. However, you and I did have a deal, and I am going to keep my end. Here's the money we agreed on. If any of that material that you have on Isaac or John," she added, pointing to the computer, "is backed up somewhere else or is retrievable or ever gets into someone else's hands, our deal is off. We will hunt you down."

As Susan reached the door and stood by John, she turned once again to address the man. "My advice to you is that, if you want to keep your business and your life intact, hide from us! Hide from us like your life depends on it."

John closed the door behind them with a sly smile on his face.

Isaac, taking one last look at the room on his way out, watched the man rub his hands on his pants and reach for his money.

Isaac was proud of his people. Susan had underestimated John, but she wouldn't again. They had both faced this problem independently and together. The fact that it was partly to honor him did not hurt his pride either. They were the team now. They were the new orphan survivors!

Isaac rushed to catch up with them.

The Truth Will Out

NEITHER JOHN NOR SUSAN KNEW exactly what to say in the elevator after they left the private investigator's office, so they let silence reign.

Once outside, Susan exclaimed, "My god! I thought you were going to *kill* him!"

John grunted, "Not here. The office."

"Good. We need to talk," she replied, still a little shocked.

As Isaac watched them, he could see that John had calmed down considerably, but he was still an angry bear of a man.

John turned his back on Susan and left her at the curb as they both walked to their respective cars.

Isaac made a snap decision. He chose to hitch a spiritual ride with Susan if only to give himself a small break from the anger and sadness of John. Isaac jumped across and anchored himself anew to Susan. He had never made an unassisted switch before and felt proud.

* * *

The switch reminded Isaac of his guide and a question that had been nagging at him since the earlier assault.

"Fella?"

"Yes, Isaac. I am here. I see that you are learning how to jump between your people."

"Can I jump and anchor to anyone?" It was not his most pressing question, but it was a good starting point. He didn't know what skills or knowledge he would need in this new world.

"No. Only your people. For you, it's John or Susan. You can detach yourself from both if you ever need to, but you can't attach to anyone else but them."

Isaac gave himself a moment to consider Fella's response before deciding that he needed one more piece to complete the puzzle. "And why, Fella, why would I want to detach from them?"

Being no longer alive himself, almost every aspect of their lives now fascinated him. Even the simple act of one of them brushing their teeth gave Isaac a longing to perform that daily task one last time to savor the experience. Given the chance, he would cherish every stroke of a brush or shower himself as if in holy water. He could now endure hours of watching them sleep only to marvel over one word mumbled aloud during a dream.

"There could be many reasons that you may wish to detach, Isaac," Fella explained. "If you needed a break, for example. Even souls get tired. Or maybe your two assigned people are not close enough for an unassisted jump, and the person you are with is doing something you don't want to see."

"I want to see *everything*."

"That's because, so far, you have seen nothing. A time will come when you will choose blindness over sight. Remember that what you see, we see. Perhaps you don't want us to see *everything*."

Isaac was getting used to Fella's riddles. He now understood that they weren't meant to sound clever or funny. Fella simply needed to consult the Many Many or consider the complexities in the answers behind each simple question.

Isaac saved this topic to ponder later and continued. "The screens, Fella. Why can't I see the computer screens?"

"I should have warned you earlier. You are becoming less like them and more like us now. It happens slowly so you have time to adjust. Technology, as you know it, is for the living and not us. Your eyes will start to see things that living people don't see, but the price you pay for that ability is digital information. Your eyes will no longer feast on that."

"What will I see instead?"

"You will see and feel life in its fullest capacity. You will see people — *your* people — like a view behind a veil. You will see them live, love, hate and perhaps even die," Fella explained. "In fact, you will do it together. You are their witness."

"Thank you, Fella. I'm starting to realize what a privilege it is. I will return to them now," Isaac said, allowing his focus to sharpen on the reality of the living.

* * *

Susan parked her car and walked into the office. It was the first time she had been back there since Isaac's death. Coming back as a rich woman and not a mere employee or prized pet of Isaac's, she commanded a different type of energy. She tried hard to hide the anxiety she felt for the difficult conversation ahead, but to Isaac it was still detectable.

When Susan and Isaac entered the old office, they found John sitting behind the desk like a child pretending to be the teacher in grade school. He pushed aside the papers he had been looking at and gestured to the seat in front.

Isaac couldn't help himself. Seeing his old playground reminded him of all the fun he'd had in that room although he had regrets about the way he had treated Susan in his first year of infatuation with his new secretary. His fond memories turned sour the moment they resurfaced, so he stopped reminiscing.

John spoke first. "You're free of him now, Susan. He knows that, if anything comes out, he'll have to face me again. Experience tells me that he won't want to do that in a hurry."

"Thank you, John," Susan said sincerely. "Although you did scare me in there. I was ready to pay. I could have just paid him off and left."

"No. He was threatening you. You can't leave a transaction like that with the other party thinking it can be repeated. He would have spent the money quickly in excitement and then come back to you demanding more. Next time, he would have been much more forceful. This way at least he'll see the bruises every day for a week or two. He'll know that you are no longer hiding it from me. That's why I had to do what I did."

John didn't wait for an acknowledgment or approval before continuing. "But now you have a new problem: *Me.* I want to know who you really are. You turned up here rather than running, which saved me coming after you, so I'm assuming that you have some story to tell. Now is your time. Start talking, and we'll see where we take it from there."

Susan seemed to be trying to figure out where to start. "Well, my name really is Susan although Mitchell was added when I was a teenager. Isaac never knew this, but you and he have known me for much longer than you think. Over twenty-seven years longer actually." She allowed a moment for the information to settle in. "We were at the orphanage together."

Isaac, forever watching, studied John's face for his reaction. He knew that, if Susan had told him this information while he was alive, the news likely would not have been received well. Outside of the brotherhood that he and John had shared in order to survive, there had been no other fond memories of their childhood home. Any reference to the orphanage would have been treated with suspicion, not open arms.

John sat like a mountain but not an unmovable one. At the mention of the orphanage, he blinked away a distaste but quickly recovered his composure. "Okay. I'm not sure how you want me to react to that news. Is it supposed to make you my sister? I don't do reunions."

Susan seemed disappointed by John's response. She looked down as if picking the words from the floor. "No, John. I don't expect you to welcome me with both arms open because of that. I'm not randomly tracking down orphans."

"Then why did you come to us? Was it the money?"

"NO!" she protested with every ounce of her body. "I've told you that."

"Then why?"

"Because, like you, it was my job to look after Isaac and you as an aside," Susan explained. When she saw John's reaction, she added, "It's true! Don't look at me like that. I got you both out of trouble without you even knowing it at least twice over the last five years."

John wasn't buying it. "So, you're supposed to be our guardian angel, are you?"

"No. I'm just repaying a debt." Her feelings were visibly hurt again but not to the extent of his previous rebuff.

John raised his voice. "*What* debt? He didn't lend you any money!"

Susan's frustration and disappointment were pasted on her face. The muscles in her neck pulled tighter than Isaac had ever seen.

"It's not about *money*, for God's sake! Why do you keep coming back to money every time?" she cried. "I did *terrible* things to get money to try and bail out Isaac, and never once did I ask for or take a cent that I did not earn from you."

John threw a mocking glare her way and replied at the same volume, "Because that's all we have to give! If it's not about money, then what is this great debt you're trying to repay Isaac and me? How have we bought this amazing loyalty from the shadows?"

Isaac could see that John was trying to intimidate the absolute truth out of her.

"YOU DIDN'T BUY MY LOYALTY!" Susan screamed.

"Then what, Susan? Why are we so lucky?"

Susan took a breath to compose herself. Then, as she was about to exhale, she allowed the words to escape her mouth. "Because Isaac killed my father."

Broken Children

JOHN WAS SHOCKED. HE TOOK a deep breath, pausing before speaking and giving the game away. "You're *crazy*! Isaac was a good man. He never killed anyone." He laughed, but it was a feeble attempt to bluff.

Susan chose her words carefully like she was walking across a suspension bridge with rotted planks. "He was a *fine* man, John. And a fine boy also. You *both* were. I'm not surprised that neither of you remembered me. I was at the orphanage. And I was there the night that Isaac killed my father. You knew him as Brother Anthony."

The forced smirk on John's face evaporated. Even Isaac had not seen this coming. He was still tethered to Susan. While he could only get a standard visual on John, he could see right into her. The Susan he saw with his new eyes was telling the truth, completely overrun by shame.

John said nothing.

Isaac had never discussed the details with John about what actually happened that night, but John had guessed the next morning. It became clear in the light of the new day with all the police onsite that someone had died, and the only person not at the scene had been Brother Anthony. It had been easier on John not knowing the details over the coming days. Isaac's ability to lie when required had never been one of John's key skills.

"I'm so very sorry for what he did to you and Isaac, John," Susan said, her voice breaking. "You don't know how long I've wanted to tell you that."

"But how is that *possible*?" John asked. "He was a *priest*! He didn't have a family."

"My mother was at the orphanage years before us, and he raped her. I know this because he took immense joy in telling me so. He rubbed it in my face at every opportunity."

"You can't believe a word he said, Susan. He said all sorts of things."

"You're right, John. But, on this occasion, it was true. Three different people from those days have confirmed it."

John was lost in thought, searching himself for how he felt about the new situation. The apology snapped him back to the room, but he said nothing.

"And I know it was Isaac because I was watching the office when it happened," Susan shuddered. "I heard the noise and saw him come out of there. I went in right after. There was blood everywhere."

"Who else knows? Isaac may be dead, but I still don't want this information to get out."

Any normal person listening to this conversation would have heard the question for what it was, but Isaac was immediately on alert. John was summing up the information and considering damage control. Isaac suddenly grew concerned for Susan's safety.

Susan, however, did not see the world as a normal person. She saw the world like John did — and like Isaac had when he was alive. To them, the world was made up of predators and prey.

"Nobody, John. If I'd wanted the world to know, I would have told them already. Hell, if I'd had the courage or the strength, I would have killed him myself. So, put those thoughts away. I am not a problem that needs to be dealt with, John Hannebery," she added, starting and finishing both sides of her own conversation and making up John's mind for him. "Okay. I sort of figured that this conversation would happen sometime. I just expected that it would be with Isaac and not you of all people."

"Well, he's gone now, so what can you tell me? What happened that night, and why were you so happy to see your father dead?"

"I can tell you some things but let me give you a little background first."

As John pushed his body back in the chair for a more relaxed listening position, he said, "Sure. Start where you want. I've got all the time in the world."

"Like I said earlier, I'm almost certain that he raped my mother, just like he raped and beat up everyone else whom he could get his fingers around. It gave him so much joy to inflict pain on others."

Susan paused, obviously unable to fathom the extent of her father's depravity, even as an adult. After a moment, she continued. "My mother was one of the girls at the orphanage before us, perhaps only 15 or 16. It's hard to tell. He finally raped someone who was old enough to have a child: me. When you suddenly have a young girl, supposedly under the protection of adult men, who gets pregnant, questions are asked.

"To deflect the attention, the staff had accused her of sleeping with some of the boys, but mostly they knew better and, by the time she was showing, it was already too late. Too many people knew. My father couldn't just kill her off, which I'm sure is what he would have wanted to do. She carried me to term and died during childbirth.

"I know this because I spoke to one of the brothers who was there at that time. He was not one of the bad ones. He left shortly after I was born. He told me that he couldn't look at me, knowing where I'd come from. He broke down in front of me the moment he started talking. For many years, I think he blamed my mother for what happened. He said that it was easier to blame her than to accept that a man of God could do what my father did. Anyway, he's not with us anymore."

"You didn't …?" John asked.

Susan smiled. "No, John. I'm not capable. I tried once though with a different guy. A real motherfucker who deserved to die, but I couldn't pull the trigger. Strange. I always thought that I probably could if I really wanted to, but it's not that easy."

John nodded. "Either have I. None that I was aware of anyway." He thought about what Susan had told him regarding Lance Rampe.

"You nearly did, John. That day you beat up Lance and left him in that state, he was close to death. You're lucky that I called an ambulance."

Isaac recalled John's mood that day. John had been frustrated by a woman he was getting close to at the time and had been in a foul mood before he left. Isaac had wondered if sending John out in that state would be a good idea. In the end, he had decided that, when the boys' type of justice needed to be enforced, it needed to be enforced right away. After all, there was no use smacking a naughty child the day after he had done something wrong. You needed to wind up that backswing and let it fly in the name of justice.

John was about to respond but Susan stopped him.

"It's okay, John. I know that you're not that kind of guy. Even Isaac wasn't really that kind of guy. He was just pushed to the breaking point at the orphanage. Instead of breaking, he decided to fight back regardless of the cost. I didn't see it happen because the door was closed, but I heard it. He may have been my biological father, but that bastard deserved everything he got. Imagine how much pain he would have kept inflicting, day after day, year after year, had Isaac not stopped him once and for all!"

Hearing the last sentence from Susan seemed to calm John's nerves.

Isaac could see the change in his posture.

"So, what's your story then?" John asked. "How the hell was Brother Anthony your father and none of us knew? I'm sorry, but I don't think I remember you at all." John scratched his head as if the act itself would help uncover his memory. "I knew the day you came in here that you were a survivor of some sort. You just had that armor. You felt like one of us."

"I'm not surprised that you don't remember me. That single trait is probably what helped me stay alive," Susan said, absolving him of his embarrassment.

Isaac considered for the briefest moment that she was using her natural voice and not the upper-class accent she had adopted for him. There was no pretense here, which was probably a good thing if she was trying to win John's trust.

Susan continued. "I must have reminded my father of my mother's death and his failure to control the situation. I specifically remember him telling me that I wasn't as much fun to hurt as the other kids. He tried to mess me up a few times, but he couldn't bring himself to do it. In the end, he just got angry and said that, if I ever got in his way, he would put his hands around my throat and squeeze until I was dead."

"That must have been a difficult thing for a child to hear."

"Yep. I was six at the time. He hadn't even touched my neck at that point, and yet I woke up the next morning with a rash around my neck that stayed for weeks."

"What did you do?"

"I hid. I hid like my life depended on it." Susan looked up in the air as if the past lay just above her head. "I stuck to the corners of rooms. I said nothing when he was around. I even missed meals if he was there. Anything to stay away and stay alive. Soon enough, I knew his patterns and worked around them. Sure, he caught me once or twice, but he seemed to be happy that I was petrified when he did."

John was listening intently, but he was starting to get physically distracted. It was as if his mind was engaged but his skin increasingly wanted to be somewhere else.

Isaac could see what was happening but wondered if Susan would pick up on it.

"Did he ever get his hands on you?"

"He didn't, John, but others did. One even told me that my father had arranged it," Susan said with tears in her eyes. "Even though that bastard didn't want to see me, I watched him. Each night, I saw him take you all into that damn torture room of his. I heard the sobs, the screams, the fucking misery that came out of that room. Through it all,

I remember feeling so sorry that, for whatever reason, he couldn't take out his anger on me. But he could on all of you. Perhaps I could have taken just one of those beatings and spared one of you a single night of pain."

"He was dishing out that pain long before you were born. You have absolutely nothing to feel sorry for," John said, rubbing his hand along the back of his neck like he was trying to start a fire. His focus was with Susan, but it was clear that a separate craving demanded more of him with every moment.

Isaac had seen John like this when they had first started making their money and women and drugs were rewards for their hard work. Isaac had been the stronger brother and had pulled them both out of the most toxic of the two addictions. This time, he couldn't grab John and shake him. Isaac leaned forward and whispered in Susan's ear. "Help him."

Susan, however, was reliving the grief of her childhood and didn't hear Isaac's request. "I know that now," she continued. "I guess I always just felt that, because we shared the same blood, I shared his guilt."

"No, you ..." John started to say, but his eyes began to drift. It was clear he was unbalanced.

Isaac repeated, "He needs your help *now*, Susan!"

Susan was about to speak again, but this time it looked to Isaac as if she may have heard him. "John, you don't look well. Should I get you to a doctor?"

"No. I think we should pick this up again tomorrow." He started to rise but had to steady himself on the edge of the desk.

Isaac watched Susan size him up. She seemed to come up with a prognosis like a professional. "I can't have you like this, John. If you and I are going to be partners, I need you to clean yourself up or at least get it under control. I have been down this path once before, and it doesn't end well if you can't control it."

John straightened himself in surprise. "Partners? What do you mean *partners?* Anyway, I'm fine. Just a little tired."

"Partners? Oh, the standard "you save me, I save you" stuff. We can talk about it tomorrow," she added, waving it away like it was no big deal. "Tonight, I need you to make me a promise."

John was staring at the door like a man waiting for the starter gun to sound. "What promise?"

"Whatever you are about to go home and take, take only half. Just get yourself through the night and come back to me tomorrow. I know that nothing I can say will stop you from taking it altogether but promise me that for now. We'll be one step closer to getting you better in the morning."

John was about to protest but must have decided that too much honesty had been shared that day to spoil it now. He simply nodded and pushed himself to his feet, looking amazed at how fast he had deteriorated on this occasion.

Susan checked him over again. "How long has whatever this is been a problem for you?"

"It only became a problem when you cared just now. Isaac kept me in check quite well, but I used to do a little extra when he wasn't watching to get me through the tough times. When he died, I guess I stopped having to hide it." He was thinking the words and saying them without a filter but through a little physical pain. "You could say that he was my anchor."

Susan considered John's words before responding. "If Isaac was your anchor, then now you are free. Firstly, you need to kick that poison out of your body — for good this time. How long can this place continue to trade without someone at the helm calling the shots? Isaac kept me out of those discussions."

"Another two weeks or so with the current portfolio. I'm not sure that I can actually run this place, you know?"

"Not like this you can't, and not by yourself. The business can wait a little longer. We have to sort you out first. Be back here tomorrow at ten a.m. John, whatever you are going to put in your system or do tonight, know this: I won't judge you — not after everything we have gone through — but, if you want me to hang around, you need to be clean of it. Take half, enjoy it, but know that it will be your last."

Isaac, forever watching and still tethered to Susan, heard and felt her words. She was taking John under her wing in the same way a child takes a bird that has fallen from its nest. It was clear that she meant what she said.

Isaac searched John's face for his response. He had never actually seen Susan talk at any length directly to John. To the best of his knowledge, the most they had ever talked to each other may have been to relay an order from him. They had been a close team, but Isaac had always been the center of it like separate spokes connected to a central hub.

He needed to hear — and feel — John's response, so he jumped across from Susan and tethered himself to John. From his new vantage point, Isaac leaned forward and whispered in John's ear, "This is your chance. Let her help you."

As usual, John gave no indication of having heard Isaac's encouragement, but he seemed to have arrived at the same conclusion anyway, saying, "Okay."

Isaac could tell that he meant it.

Not All Broken Things Can Be Repaired

———•———

SOMETHING WAS NOT RIGHT WITH John. Isaac could feel it the moment he jumped across. It felt like drinking a big gulp of sour milk. He felt it in the pit of his stomach or where it would have been if he'd still had one.

As he was carried from the room on the back of John, Isaac allowed himself a final glance at Susan. She was still beautiful but not in the lustrous way that he had always seen her. Instead, it was because of the things that she had been through and survived. He was seeing a strength in her that he didn't know she was capable of. Concern for John still lingered in her eyes. Tears were still wet on her cheeks, and her held breath was caught in the grip of her throat. All these things screamed, "I am living. I am beautiful." Unfortunately for Isaac, they reminded him that he was neither.

* * *

"Fella?" Isaac asked in a tired tone over his right shoulder. "Are you there?"

"Yes, Isaac. I am here."

"Did you know any of this, Fella? Did you know that Brother Anthony was Susan's father?"

"Yes. We — the Many Many — knew that specifically but not all of it. We are learning anew with your witness. You are filling some gaps for us."

"Can you tell me what is wrong with John? Something feels very wrong there."

"We can never know what is to come with the living, only what has been. The future is theirs to create, and the past is ours to contemplate. You must witness him for us to know anything."

Isaac sighed. In a weary tone, he said without thought or motive, "Thank you for being my guide." It was comforting to have a voice that still acknowledged his existence.

"Isaac, being your guide is my privilege."

* * *

Isaac tuned back into John, who was pulling into the driveway of his house. He got out of the car like a man whose every muscle screamed in pain and made his way into the house.

Isaac had expected John to take some kind of drug before leaving the office, but he hadn't. This inaction screamed alarm and told Isaac that John wasn't after a short-term fix. He was preparing himself for something big.

John fumbled with the lock on his own front door for much longer than a simple drunk might have done. He even seemed to consider kicking down the door at one point, but then seemed to remember that the rich protect themselves with the best that money can buy. Their doors are not easily opened and are never broken. After five minutes of pure determination, John was in. He went straight to the room where Isaac had witnessed him with his gun pressed to his temple the day before. It had been cleaned, which John didn't seem to notice.

"Whoever John's cleaner is, she is amazing!" Isaac thought, allowing one moment of humor to steady himself for what was ahead.

John retrieved a laptop and brought it to the dining table. He didn't agonize through its startup process but instead went to a drawer and fetched a small, black plastic bag and a pair of headphones. Satisfied that he had all he needed for the job ahead, he sat behind the computer, which was completing its wake from hibernation.

Isaac tried to look over John's shoulder at the screen. As before, the screen showed him a blurred light with no detail. It was like trying to read a newspaper through a tear.

John snapped the headphones around his head and plugged the cable into the computer. These were the sort of headphones that only the rich owned. He pinched his nose with one hand and rubbed his elbow with the other.

Isaac could feel an anxiety enter the room like smoke.

John reached for the black plastic bag and poured its contents onto the table. As Isaac had expected, a dozen small bags of white power silently dropped out. John made a motion to grab for them but then held himself back.

Isaac jumped at this chance. "Half," he whispered hurriedly into John's ear.

As usual, it was unclear if John had heard. Regardless, John divided up the small bags, pushing roughly half aside with his forearm and sweeping them back into the black plastic bag.

Isaac was impressed that John didn't count out exactly

half. He had either valued Susan's wishes or simply been too affected to care. Either way, he had kept his promise.

John zipped up the black plastic bag and threw it across the room in the general direction of where it had come. He then prepared neat tracks of glistening white crystal. It looked appealing, even to a soul who no longer had the body to consume it. John took a $50 bill from his wallet and invited the drug into his system. He took it in and held it, ensuring that none of the crystal could find its way back out. To be doubly sure it stayed within his system, John pinched the end of his nose.

Isaac's tether to John was not just for anchorage. He felt the drug the moment John did but without the physical sensation. There was no bitter aftertaste, no blocked sinus and no initial dissolve. Even though it was not completely unpleasant, it gave him a fizzle that he had never felt before, but it still felt like an unnatural corruption.

John didn't give himself time to reconsider. He took the second line and repeated the process of trapping it within his system. One by one, the lines vanished, and he immediately pulled the laptop close and started typing.

Isaac had seen all of this before with John but never this quantity or consumed at this speed. He would usually take this amount over four or five hours at a party. The other thing that Isaac noticed was that the drugs seemed to be a secondary concern. They were clearly necessary for his function but were not his primary directive: courage to face what was next. No matter how hard he tried, Isaac could get no focus on whatever was on the computer.

It was clear that John was searching for something. He typed a few words, pressed return and sat back, considering the results the computer fed him. Isaac saw him scrolling through pages of blurred text and images. Then, it seemed as if John had found his content.

Although this search success should have made John happy, it didn't. The anger that had been in him since the bashing he had dished out earlier that day found focus and intensity. It was as if a magnifying glass had brought itself to the very point where the sun's rays could start a fire.

Anger wasn't all that Isaac felt. A new feeling crept into the room like a competing stench trying to drown out another. Isaac didn't know if it was the drugs finding a home in John's bloodstream and then onto Isaac through his anchorage, or a new unique sensation visiting through an emotional back door. It was alive, pungent and suffocating.

Isaac searched John's face for a clue to what he saw on the computer screen. At first, Isaac saw nothing. Then John subtly rubbed the back of his arm along his crotch. If he had simply been tuning into porn, Isaac was sure that he would have felt it differently. Something about the situation felt wrong. A shit-soup of emotion circled around John, and lust was just the conduit.

Isaac wanted to leave but not just yet. He had no intention of waiting around to watch John masturbate, but something about the situation did not fit right. He needed to see it before he felt comfortable enough to leave.

John did not seem entirely happy with his viewing and reached up to adjust the headphones. He switched them on, and an abundance of excess sound filled their heads.

Isaac listened for clues for what might be on the screen.

John continued to allow his forearm to breathe life into whatever was beneath his jeans.

The high-pitched squeeze was not the heavy breathing that Isaac expected to hear. He wondered if perhaps he could not hear the electronic sounds in the same way that he could not see the screens, but there was a slight familiarity with the sound that told him it was not the case.

Although the sound was excessively loud, John did not reach to quiet it. Instead, hearing it burst into his eardrums seemed to enhance his experience. His eyes shone brightly as if the excessive sound had nowhere to go but in through his ears and out through his retinas.

"What is that sound?" Isaac asked himself. "Steal grinding on steal? Amplified fingernails assaulting a chalkboard?" For four seconds, the sound persisted without identity, and then its pitch started to waver. To Isaac's horror, everything made sense all at once. John's senses had been drowned in adrenaline by the sound of a child's scream.

During a brief respite in the sound, Isaac imagined the child turning red and shaking as its emotion overtook its capacity to breathe. Then, the next scream exploded into the room — from the initial breath ... to the voice box ... to the stratosphere.

"Oh, my god," Isaac thought.

The intensity in John's eyes burned like an inferno and his hands fumbled with his crotch.

Isaac swung himself around to face John eye to eye. "*How,* John? After everything we went through?"

While John's excitement was clearly evident, there was something else there: shame. John blinked as his eyes watered. He was fighting an internal battle and losing.

Isaac was fighting his own battle. It occurred to him that, if he could see John in this fashion, then the Many Many could do the same. His everlasting loyalty to John outweighed his anger at the situation. He would let John fight this battle alone and away from the eyes of others.

Isaac tried to jump off John. He was able to clear himself for a moment, but — with no new anchor — he fell back into John's sphere just in time to hear the slap of a hand on skin and a child renew his sorrowed outrage. Isaac tried to jump again but found himself sucked back into the room. He jumped and jumped, always landing back into John's orbit with a thud every time.

John seemed to notice this impact, blinking and nodding his head ever so slightly each time. However, it did not seem to distract his attention from the horrors of his agonizing pleasure. New screams filled their heads as John's headphones broadcasted the misery in the best clarity that money could buy.

The child's voice was gone. Isaac thought that perhaps John was watching a compilation of child abuse. Slap and scream, slap and scream, scrolling like a child misery merry-go-round. As Isaac's entire being was the sum of his memories and thoughts, held together with a little cosmic glue, he didn't have the luxury of distracting himself from the situation. Every scream became a personal living nightmare.

* * *

"Fella! FELLA? I need you. Get me *out* of here!" Isaac screamed. He didn't wait for a reply and was close to hysterical. "Fella! Fe …"

Isaac's lights went out, and he was once again suspended within the embrace of an alternate universe.

"I have you, Isaac," Fella said calmly. "You are safe now."

Isaac cried without tears and without sobbing, but he cried just the same — the way a soul cries in the dark, in agony, in shame, but also in relief.

After he had taken time to recover, he finally spoke. "What did you see, Fella?"

"Only what you saw, Isaac. No more and no less."

Isaac wasn't ready for his oldest and greatest friend's soul to be judged. "And them? The Many Many! What did they see?"

"They see and hear only what you and I do."

"Then they have nothing!" Isaac said, surprising himself.

"Perhaps not."

Isaac took a few moments to allow his anger to drain. He only had one friend in this reality and, with the latest discovery about John's and Susan's double lives, he felt further from them than ever before. He didn't want to lose everyone.

"Fella, has he ... has he ever *done* anything to a child?"

Fella didn't answer right away. Isaac had the impression that he was rewinding through a lifetime, looking for the answer. "No, Isaac. I don't believe that he has ever touched a child personally. If he had, we would know."

"But how can you be so sure, Fella? You never saw me."

"You, Isaac, were a child born without a mother. Your mother died before you were taken from her body. It would be many years before anyone looked upon you with love. That is the only reason we didn't see you. The chances of that happening are rare. You are a special case. I have reviewed all the memories of John's life so far. I see no child suffering at his hands other than when he was a child himself. And most of that was at your request."

"Okay. Thank you. That makes sense. Then why? Why does he watch it?"

"The answer seems to be in the violence. It triggers something in him. As you know, we can't see *within* the living. We only witness the lives that they *live*."

"What happens now? How do I know when it's safe to go back?"

Fella seemed to think before responding. "He has finished the action that upset you."

"What is next?"

"He will likely sob in shame for around forty-five minutes before screaming out aloud that he will never do it again." After a pause, Fella continued. "But he likely will."

"How do we fix him?"

"We can't."

"He was my only friend. I can't accept that."

"Your job is to witness. Perhaps, if he is lucky, the next time he is holding a gun to his head, you will be there once again to whisper in his ear."

Isaac allowed the implied responsibility behind Fella's words sink in. It gave weight to his very existence.

"Based on his past behavior, do you think that he will be putting a gun to his head tonight?"

"No. It is unlikely tonight, Isaac. He has too much rage in his despair."

"Good. Can you please send me to Susan? I can't see John right now."

The New Day

B Y THE TIME ISAAC WAS sent to Susan's immediate orbit
the night before, she was already asleep. After his heart-
breaking discovery at John's house earlier, Isaac embraced
the peace and allowed his vision to feast on the beauty of her
being.

It occurred to him that he might be invading Susan's privacy by being ever present, but two things allowed him to
make peace with the notion. Firstly, she had seemed to know
that he was there and had even found peace in his presence.
She had heard his voice when he whispered and had even
tuned him out when she wanted to.

The other reason that Isaac made peace with his soul-
stalking of Susan was his suspicion that, without her and
John, he simply would not exist. While Fella had told Isaac
that their existence depended on his witness, Isaac was starting to get a feel for the new world around him and the chain
of existence. Susan required his witness. Isaac needed Fella's guidance. Fella had the backing and the resources of the
Many Many. Beyond that was anyone's guess.

* * *

When his two people came together on this new day, it was different. They had been through something together; secrets had been shared and blood had been drawn. They now shared a new bond. They were in Isaac's old office, but it no longer gave Isaac the same sense of power. It was theirs now. The new owners gave it an essence all their own.

Given that he was much bigger than Isaac, John sat in Isaac's old chair differently. John's physical size commandeered the seat rather than commanding it the way Isaac had. To John, it was an office chair in the top offices; to Isaac, it had been a throne.

Looking around the room, Isaac surprised himself with the once-so-important and now irrelevant information that sprang to mind. "That chair cost $7,000! John sits on it like it's a milk crate. That desk was $23,000! That picture cost half a mill..."

Susan was the first to say something of importance, so Isaac tuned in.

"John, you made me a promise yesterday. Before we start, I need to know if I *can trust you.*" She let the last three words linger in disgust.

"That's what I promised, and that's what I did. Believe me, if I had taken all that I had intended to take last night, we would not be talking right now. But, right now, I am in a major hole, and it's about more than just drugs. I'm a broken man, and I'm not sure that everything broken can be fixed. You should know that."

"Oh, I do," Susan replied. "But, John, you need to know this: The world is not done with you yet, and neither am I."

Susan's words rang like poetry into Isaac's ears, but they needed to be more than just words or John would eventually turn on her. Even in this state, John would not be easily led by another person. Isaac searched the smile that Susan had now brandished and found no hint of insincerity. It shone brightly in the darkness in the way only love for another can. They were like siblings now.

"Talk to me, John. You helped me out yesterday, and now I would like to try and help you if I can."

John's head was clearly foggy from his consumption the night before, but he was not completely gone. He cleared his throat and took a deep breath before he spoke. "Well, as you can probably tell, I have not been coping well since Isaac's death."

It was said as a statement, but it landed in Isaac's ears as an accusation. "He blames me for leaving him," Isaac thought.

"You could say that his death has brought up some old demons. Your wonderful father and his friends actually." John sensed Susan's reaction and added, "No, wait … before you say anything, it's okay. I don't hold you responsible for what he did to us. It's just that I never got my closure."

"*Closure?* He's dead, isn't he? What more do you want?"

"I know that, but I didn't get to kill him. While Isaac was still alive, it didn't seem to matter. Now that he's dead, it does. Whenever I close my eyes, your father is there, waiting for me. And none of this …" John gestured to his muscle-packed body, "none of this matters. I'm just a scared little boy again."

Isaac had never heard John speak in this way before. Perhaps it was because he had never asked specifically about the situation. Perhaps it was because it required a woman's touch to ply this truth from his mouth. Or perhaps he had never cared enough for the answer to set it free. Either way, it shamed Isaac to consider it now.

Susan seemed at a loss for words, but she tried anyway. "*Scared?* I thought you were so brave, John. Whenever Isaac sent me on an errand, I would ask myself, 'How would John handle this?'"

"Then I am the bravest coward I know. I just know how to hurt people."

Susan let his words hang in the air. They held weight in the room. Isaac could feel them on his essence before they dissolved into the universe forever.

"I'm going to help you, John," Susan replied quietly after a few moments. She wasn't sure of the words, but Isaac could see something forming behind her eyes like a seed that needed time to grow. "Oh, don't worry! I'm not talking about some shrink. People like you and me, John, don't heal like normal people. We break, and then evolve into the people we become next. Stronger people. Your story is not written yet, John Hannebery."

"What do you have in mind?"

"One final task to set you free. You'll be born again, and a light will shine in your darkness once more. Let me ask you this: Do you need to make any more money?"

"No. Isaac made sure of that. To be honest, I never cared for it anyway. I never seem to know what to do with it."

"And the business itself? What does it mean to you?"

"Nothing without Isaac."

This answer seemed to make Susan happy. "Good. Then it's settled. I am going to give you the one thing you are missing. A mission."

"A *mission?* What sort of mission?"

"We'll get to that later. I have some research to do first, which may take me a few weeks. In the meantime, I need a favor. While this business might not mean anything to you, it does to me. It reminds me of Isaac, and I think that I would like to run it in his honor. I want it to be *my* mission."

To Isaac's surprise, John didn't hesitate. "It's yours. I'll sign it over right now."

"No, John, not yet. I have some things to attend to first. I want you to run it for me for the time being. Don't worry. Only for a few weeks. Then, once I have the information I need, we can exchange. Can you do that for me, John? Do I need to get you into rehab, or can you keep it together for a few weeks? Just pretend that Isaac is on a holiday and that you're managing it until he and that dirty whore secretary of his comes back." Susan allowed the delicious naughtiness of the old accent she'd kept for Isaac to make an appearance.

"You were never a dirty whore to me, Susan. I knew the moment I first saw you that you were one of us. I didn't recognize you, but I knew it just the same," John insisted.

"Thank you, John. We're all we've got. Do you accept my proposal?"

"Yes. Do what you need to do. I'll keep this place — and myself — together."

Susan smiled, pleased with herself. "Wonderful!" She reached into her handbag and produced a slip of paper. "Oh, and here's a new customer for the books. A bank manager who is very motivated to give you his money once you tell him that I sent you. Now," Susan said, standing and collecting her things, "if you will excuse me, I have some very exciting work to do."

"Are you going to tell me *anything* about what you're up to?" John asked, echoing Isaac's sentiment.

Susan smiled. "No. I don't think so. It'll be more fun this way. We need to bring a little more fun into our lives."

As she headed for the door, she paused as she passed John, who was still sitting. Then she did something that took both John and Isaac by complete surprise. She bent down and kissed John on the head. It was not a passionate kiss, but there was a moment of tenderness in it.

The kiss started a chemical reaction in John, which spread from the point of impact right through his body in an instant.

"Look after yourself, John. A big challenge is coming, a lot of responsibility, and I will need you at your best." She left the room without waiting for a response.

Without a moment's hesitation, Isaac jumped. Wherever Susan was going or whatever she was about to do, he wanted to be part of it. He felt himself pull clear of John's orbit and, for a moment, was completely unburdened in midflight. When he tried to anchor to Susan, he found no purchase. Just like in his last desperate attempt to jump clear of John, it seemed that the in-between space of his people was off limits. He immediately felt the immense pull of a cord and sprang back to John. It happened so fast that it left him dizzy and confused.

Isaac gathered his senses and attempted the leap once again, figuring that Susan should still be within his reach. Once again, he cleared John's orbit. Instead of grabbing ahold of Susan's gravity, he was hit by a wall as physical as any he had ever felt in the real world. The thud from the rejection was greater than his earlier disorientation, and his vision swum in his eyes. This new impact, followed by the rapid spring of the return flight, left him feeling disorientated.

* * *

"Fella?" he asked, struggling with the word.

"Yes, Isaac," came the now familiar voice.

"What's *wrong* with me?"

"Nothing. You will recover within moments. These leaps can be difficult at first."

"Okay. Give me a moment, and then can you please anchor me to Susan?"

"No," Fella said flatly, offering nothing else.

"Why?"

"Because she does not want you with her right now, Isaac."

"What? She knows I'm here? She can *choose*? Why didn't you tell me this before, Fella?"

"You never asked, Isaac. As I said to you once, we have lots of answers in heaven. Some answers we don't even have questions for. Perhaps you should be asking another question instead — like why she doesn't want you with her."

If Isaac had a body, he would have felt the tendons throughout his neck tighten. Instead, he tore at the energy around him like a puppet getting tangled in his own strings. "Okay. Why?"

Fella did not share in his frustration. "I don't know. We only know what is or has been. I can't know what is going on in her mind, and neither can you. That is why we watch. We watch to see the world that they create around themselves."

"But John's dream! I saw his dream, remember? *That* was in his head."

Fella's answer wasn't automatic on this occasion. "That's different. He was asleep, and it was a dream. You really shouldn't have been there. The difference is that, in the dream ..."

Isaac was stunned. It was the first time that he had heard Fella stumble on anything.

Fella changed his tack. "This is hard because there is too much for you to understand first for me to give you the full answer. Let me just say that seeing into that dream was like you and John both watching the same television set. You were not seeing him but only a projection of his thoughts."

"I'm confused," Isaac said, mentally exhausted and still a little dizzy from his rejection.

"You have only been with us for a heartbeat, Isaac. You can't understand the universe by studying a grain of sand. Knowledge is built from scratch by asking the right questions in the right order."

"Well, if Susan doesn't want me around, where does that leave me?"

"Go where you are needed, Isaac. John is going to need a lot of your guidance in the coming weeks. Help him. He will be asking, 'What would Isaac do here?' You will tell him in your whispers. Do not worry. Susan will need you again."

"Okay," Isaac said, a little calmer and more assured. He let the tension around him float away. "Please return me to John."

John by Remote Control

FOR THE NEXT TWO WEEKS, Isaac never left John's side. He was happy to be there, but it wasn't his first preference. Susan was out there somewhere, doing something interesting, while John was in the office doing more of the same. The glow of the unknown outshone the mundane. When your very existence is the sum of your thoughts, it is not easy having them divided.

Attending to the daily activities of his old business from beyond the grave no longer carried any of the allure it once had for Isaac. Success had always been about the money and the power it brought. Now, none of it had any value to him — or, it seemed, to John.

The one upside that did come out of the experience was his newfound connection to John. With the drugs no longer flooding his system, he heard Isaac's whispers better and began to listen for them.

On many occasions, John would sit back in his chair and display the face that said, "What would Isaac do in this situation?"

Isaac would then lean in and whisper, "Double down. This investment has not run its full course yet."

On one specific occasion when the question was asked, Isaac responded in frustration, "Read it out loud, John! I can't see your screen."

To Isaac's immense surprise, that is exactly what John did!

Three simple actions — hearing, listening and watching — brought the two of them together as brothers again. Even if John didn't specifically know that Isaac was there, he must have felt it. If not in his presence, then at least in his happiness.

John may have been just going through the motions, but with Isaac's guidance he did almost everything right. The only time he came unstuck was when he reverted back, unguided, to his old self. His leadership and decision-making skills were almost nonexistent. When Isaac planted an idea in John's mind, he was fine. However, left to his own resources, John's river ran dry. He would never be the natural leader that Isaac was, and Isaac knew that he could not make every decision for him by proxy.

While John's days were sunny, his nights continued to be dark, falling back to the places where Isaac could not reach him no matter how hard he tried. The drugs, with quantities much lower than before, didn't break the connection between the brothers, but they did signal that John was not willing to take Isaac's call right now.

Isaac watched his friend numb his senses and wrestle with the demons of his nightmares. Isaac had even tried to travel into one of John's dreams again, but Fella had politely declined the request, even after Isaac had offered money.

"No, Isaac," Fella had responded. "There is nothing new to learn there. Your request has been considered by the

Many Many but declined on this occasion. Your money will not make a difference this time around."

* * *

At one point during the first week, John's phone rang. Isaac had completely ignored all other calls but, after hearing one word from John, everything changed.

"Susan?" John said, happily surprised.

It was the first time that Susan and John had spoken since she had disappeared, and Isaac was desperate to be a part of it. He brought himself as close to the phone as he could before John changed ears. Isaac was unsure if his immediate presence had created the change, so he distanced himself a little further and rotated to the now active ear.

"John," Susan said. "I hope that you're looking after yourself and that business of mine." The usual chocolate tone of her voice was now metallic in this telephonic form like an AM radio slightly off station but just clear enough for Isaac to make out her words.

"Technology is for the living," he recalled Fella once telling him. Isaac was happy with what he had been served.

"I am, Susan. The business is animated again. Our investments are still strong, and we have some time before we need to make our next moves. But ... but that time will come, and you and I are not qualified to make that call. We have a few weeks tops."

"Can you start making a short list of candidates whom we could hire? And a list of our biggest competitors? I want to know which of them are most like Isaac was. This company is a shark, not a fish. We want a predator making our financial calls."

John scratched his head. "It's funny that you say that. You know. I wasn't sure if I should share this with you, but the one person most like Isaac was actually the guy who put the investigator onto us: Phillip Black. If there was going to be a list, he would be on it."

"I met him once," Susan shared. "He came to see Isaac. How do you know that he put the private investigator onto you and Isaac?"

"I saw his name on the investigator's computer when we were in his office."

"But you told him that you didn't want to know."

"That's because I already did, and I figured that it was probably best if he wasn't aware that I knew. At least that way he wouldn't see me coming when I smash him up," John said, a little too pleased with himself.

"No, John. You leave this one to me," Susan said quickly. "You will have ample opportunity to get your hands dirty."

"Ah, this grand plan of yours. Are you ready to tell me what it is?"

"No, I'm not ready to share it with you and Isaac yet. But don't worry. I'm almost done. It will be my gift to you for all the things you both did for me," Susan added with a smile in her voice, digitally corrupted for Isaac.

John's tone mellowed. "You talk about him like he's still here."

"I know he is, John. I guess that's why I haven't been missing him so much. Anyway, I gotta go. Remember what I said. Don't bother going after Phillip Black. Leave him to me. You just look after that company of mine till I get back."

"Yep. I ain't going anywhere," John said before the line went dead.

* * *

Isaac didn't waste a moment. "Fella?"

The voice resonated in his ears immediately. "No, Isaac. She is not ready for you. She wants her privacy right now. You need to respect it."

"Do I have a choice, Fella?"

"No."

Just like the phone line a moment ago, Isaac and Fella's conversation had been terminated. He considered calling Fella back but knew that nothing would come of it. These were the new rules of the jungle, and he would have to play by them.

Isaac leaned in near John's right ear once again and whispered, "Back to work."

Any living person watching at that moment would have seen John, as if by his own accord, snap himself out of a daydream and bring his attention back to the figures on his computer.

The Return of
Susan Mitchell

———•———

IT TOOK FIVE WORKING DAYS for Susan to show herself to the boys again. She turned up the following Tuesday, completely unannounced. During that time, Isaac's ability to focus on the business had decreased rapidly. He was a being of vision and feeling now, not thought. The energy it required to think through a situation and suggest a course of action to John was beyond him. Luckily, John had started to develop his own skills during the same time frame. The baton was being passed from master to apprentice, and neither of them were happy about it.

When she finally walked in, Susan's light shone in all directions like a diamond and broke the silence. "Hello, boys!" Her hair fell with a hint of a curl to frame her jawline, and her golden dress projected rays like the sun.

Isaac once again basked in her glory and, without a moment's hesitation, jumped from John to Susan like an excited puppy. When he was in flight, he considered that he might be rejected again. But, to his joy, it was not the case. He caught her orbit and spun around it like a revolving ball going down a funnel. He reached out to try and touch her skin. He knew that he probably shouldn't, but he couldn't help himself.

To Isaac's surprise, Susan took the impact physically — or, at the very least, emotionally with an effect. She had been leaning her head against the door frame when she arrived, but the impact of Isaac's anchor knocked her off balance slightly.

As she gripped for the door frame, she giggled. "Wow! It's nice to be missed."

John looked up, expecting to see another visitor to justify the dialog that seemed to have started without him. When he saw nothing, confusion crossed his face but didn't live there long. "Susan! It's great to see you. You certainly know how to make an entrance."

Susan swung Isaac around her neck like a scarf and walked them both into the room, taking her seat. She was different somehow. Isaac couldn't put his finger on it, but her elements had changed. The chemicals that made up her soul were still on the surface, but there were new, unknown elements or factions fighting for their place in her cocktail. Not all of it was pleasant. Isaac could tell that right away. But most of it was, and the rest he didn't care about. You simply take your friends, your lovers, your family and the good with the bad and accept them with love.

"How are you, John? Have you been looking after yourself like you promised me you would?" she said with a warm smile, which seemed to suggest that she already knew the answer she was seeking.

John took a step back and invited Susan to inspect for herself. "You tell me. Do I look better than when you left me?"

"You do, and I can't tell you how much joy it brings me."

Isaac took the moment to view John from his new vantage point. It was true. His old friend did look good. He knew from watching him that the drugs had been dialed back dramatically. Over the last two weeks, he had witnessed John transform from suicidal addict to businessman. It was not a comfortable transition, but it was a positive transformation nonetheless.

John and Susan looked at each other, smiling for a few moments. They were each other's only equal.

John broke the silence first. "So, I'm *dying* to know. Where have you been all this time?"

"Research, John. Research," Susan answered. The smile stayed on her face, but a personal gravity found its way into her expression. "I have an incredible gift for you but, once I give it, I can't take it back. Quite frankly, I don't know how much you are going to like it."

"Okay. Let's see it then."

Susan perked up. "Not yet. I'm going to let you buy me lunch first. Somewhere really good with lots of wine, where they only serve rich people. Besides, I want to hear all about your gift to me first. This business. What shape is it in, and when can I have it?" She pushed herself back in their chair and crossed her legs to listen.

"You're stalling," John said with the face of a child who has just been told he can't open his presents until after dinner.

"I am. Let's just take the next few hours to pretend that you and I are normal people, and then I will give you my gift in all its glory. Just remember that sometimes not getting what you want is a wonderful stroke of luck. Somebody famous said that once." Susan took a breath and smiled through a frown. "Work with me here. It's going to take some courage. Tell me about this business."

John conceded and grabbed for a ledger book, which Isaac had quietly suggested that he keep. It had proved successful on two accounts. Firstly, it had enabled Isaac to actually see the numbers now that computer screens were off limits to him. Secondly, the physical act of writing down trading positions had allowed the information to have a solid foundation in John's head to build from.

"The business is good. Isaac left us with a portfolio that could sit idle for a few months without any serious drawbacks. It won't take much to run the office but, at some point in the next few months, we will need to either readdress some of our positions or close up shop."

Susan waved him away. "Oh, we're *never* going to do that. No, this was his baby, and I'm going to run it for him as long as I possibly can. I've already arranged for someone to help out."

"Who?" John demanded, not wanting to hold onto the business but not quite ready to let it go to just anyone either.

"Phillip Black," Susan replied calmly.

"Him? I still need to pay him a little visit for hiring that investigator."

Isaac's orbit of Susan was tighter than normal and certainly tighter than he had ever had with John, but he used the moment to push himself slightly away and study her face in the hope that she might be joking.

Susan's voice was firm. "John, you will do no such thing. We had an agreement. The business will be mine to do with as I wish. I promise you that I will honor Isaac every single day that the front door is open, but to do that I need someone like him at the helm. Phillip Black is as close as I could get."

"But why *him*? I made you a list of candidates."

"And none of them would have been right. Phillip is not like normal people. He is not us but close, and through it all he survives. I've checked him out thoroughly." Susan paused, clearly trying to decide if she should say what was to come next. "I don't expect you to be happy about this right away, my friend, but let's give him a try. The fact that it makes you angry is a bonus for this afternoon. Now, how about that lunch?"

Isaac turned to study John. In the space of a few moments, at least three separate emotions flashed across his face before he settled.

"Okay, Susan. Let me tell our new personal assistant that we'll be out to lunch."

Susan smiled even larger than before. "No need. I fired her on my way in. She's not one of us, John. We want fighters and survivors."

"You *fired* her? Of course, you did. You are becoming more and more like Isaac every day."

"I think that I always was, John. It just wasn't my turn to take the reins yet. Now, grab your jacket and let's go. I'm starving!"

John stood and put on his suit jacket, righting it into the corners of his shoulders and pulling the ends of his sleeves through. It was the first time that Isaac had even seen him address his own appearance in that manner.

Susan noticed the extra effort also and gestured up and down his body. "I *like* this! This is just the start, John. You are going to become the man you were bred to be."

John, who wasn't used to compliments, struggled to find the right reply. "Ah … thank you." The thought of a woman finding him attractive was a foreign concept to him. He was about to reply through a sheepish grin when Susan stopped him.

"I love you, John, but you can forget *that* right away."

John's cheeks exploded in red, and he laughed. "Even if I pay for lunch?"

"Sorry, John. My days of giving blow jobs in exchange for a meal are truly behind me. I'm a rich woman now. Haven't you heard?"

"I know, I know. I think I liked you better in the old days. Now you're always telling me what to do!"

Susan smacked John on the back of the head, and all three left the room laughing.

The Mission, Should He Choose to Accept It

———·———

JOHN AND SUSAN'S LUNCH WAS a cocktail of old Isaac memories, business talk and general banter about other guests of the restaurant. When the alcohol had finally found its place in their systems, they decided to play a game of "How did *that* table make their money?"

"Banking," John said with a smirk. "You can always tell a banker by his suit. Rich and opulent but conservative. They live and work within a system. Real, unencumbered money comes with an 'I don't give a fuck' attitude."

"Is that what we have, John? Unencumbered money?"

"Sort of. Only we didn't make it personally. Isaac did. I guess that now he's dead, it is unencumbered, but it felt like we were both his employees. I still don't really know how to spend it. I've got no family to spoil and no vacation I've been dreaming about. I've already got all the expensive toys I could possibly need."

"Could you ever see yourself having a family, John?" Susan

asked before taking another great gulp of white wine. This question needed its own false courage as it changed the entire tone of their lunch. Their second $700 bottle was nearly empty.

"No," John said flatly with a hint of anger.

"And why is that?"

Isaac was watching Susan closely. To him, she already seemed to know the answer. The only reason that she would ask this question would be if she were walking him down a path. Isaac purged all their previous banter and focused his attention on what was to come next. Life happens in moments, and this was potentially about to be one of the important ones.

John had not hurried his answer. "Because I am broken, Susan. As much as I would like to have a beautiful woman and lovely children around me, I would find some way to hurt them. Maybe not physically, although I could not rule that out, but I would find a way. And you know why that is?"

Susan didn't respond.

"Because I hurt people. It's what I do best. I like to feel them break in my hands, the same way that I was broken so many years ago." As John spoke, his anger began to rise. Although it was not aimed at Susan, it visited their table just the same. Anger now spoke for John and through John.

"Why?" Susan asked, still pushing for a deeper truth.

John exploded, allowing his anger to play its full hand. "I want to smash them off their righteous fucking pedestals and drag them all down into the mud and filth with me!" He reached for his wine glass and, with a shaking hand, drank it deeper and harder than he had before that lunch.

Isaac and Susan sized up this new John. He grabbed his napkin, used it to wipe his mouth and then scrunched it hard within his powerful right hand. In the previous week, Isaac had not seen this John Hannebery, although he had been with him every moment of that time.

"How many, John? How many people must you hurt before you get your justice?" Susan asked quietly, obviously not wanting to inflame the situation past the current point.

"I will never have justice for what they did to me."

Susan grabbed his hand. "That's because you're hurting the wrong people!"

This was not the answer that John was expecting. "But your father is dead. Isaac killed him. Who *else* am I supposed to hurt?"

Susan maintained direct eye contact. "He was just the tip of the iceberg."

"How do you know?"

Susan took a quick drink before proceeding. "I already told you that my father didn't like messing with me like he did with you boys."

"Not as much fun, I think you said," John replied unenthusiastically.

"Exactly. Well, that didn't stop him from loaning me out to others. Over a period of three years, between the ages of four and seven, he gave me to 13 men, all of whom were either connected to the orphanage or simply rich enough to make a large contribution to it or to him."

Isaac and John were stunned. Susan was no longer the same woman who had been at the table minutes earlier.

"He gave you — his own child —to 13 men to do what-ever they pleased with you?" John asked, more to himself. He obviously had no intention of having Susan repeat the statement.

Susan reached into her handbag and produced a folded piece of ruled paper. She slid it across the table and under John's fingers. At the same time as the paper reached the back of his palm, Susan grabbed his hand. The paper and its written secrets were his, but she was not quite ready to reveal their message.

Susan continued to hold John's hand as she spoke. "John, my father stole your childhood and your entire life's happiness. Isaac gave you safety, but in doing so also took your vengeance. Anger and shame run in your veins, and no matter how many people you hurt over trivial money matters, your thirst for vengeance will never be satisfied. Do you understand that?"

"What would you have me do, Susan? *Therapy?* I'm not sure that I am fixable."

"I don't want to fix you, John. I want to *refine* you," Susan explained, allowing her thumb to stroke the top of his hand. "I want to take all of your rage, which they put in you, and give it focus. I want to give your life meaning again!"

"How?" John asked, suddenly uneasy.

"They say that you need to kill your demons before they kill you."

John cut her off. "I told you before that I've *never* killed anyone!"

"Oh, but you *could*, John! I've seen you hurt people. I've seen their bones break in your hands and the look in your eyes when they do. You will never be able to murder the man who hurt you. Isaac already saved us all from him.

"Perhaps I can give you the next best thing." Susan paused and then continued, raising the index finger of her left hand. "My first gift to you, although you may not see it that way now, is my most precious. I am gifting you my anger, hatred and loathing of my father and every one of those bastard motherfuckers who put their dirty hands on me when I was a child. I can't live with the anger anymore, and I'm not violent enough to give it any satisfaction. I will never be able to have a future if I carry that poison around with me."

John still looked a little confused.

"However, you must understand that with this first gift comes a responsibility on your part," Susan continued. "I can only be free of my anger if I know that it will be avenged. That is why I have a second gift."

She squeezed John's hand with the paper still underneath and lifted another finger. "My second gift is this list. On it, you will find the names and last known addresses of the remaining 9 of the 13 men who assisted my father, sanctioned or profited from his behavior or personally put their hands on me. I want you to take all that beautiful anger and rage, which you have bottled up inside, and all the extra that I have just given you and become a weapon of retribution."

John removed his hand from under hers, withdrawing the note.

Isaac studied John's face and understood that he was not ready to respond to Susan yet. Perhaps John thought that it might be some kind of joke, one where showing your enthusiasm too soon would make you the punchline. He studied the paper before closing it up and placing it down on the table.

"I told you. I've never killed anyone," John said sadly.

"And I believe you," Susan said, again grasping for his hand.

On this occasion, John pulled it away.

Susan continued. "I also know that you have the potential,

and two weeks ago I am quite sure that you were about to kill yourself. I heard some of it in your voice on the phone, but without a doubt I saw it in your eyes the following day. If so, it may have been your gun, but your demons were about to pull the trigger, John. I think it's only fair that, before you help them finish off what they started, you might try and even up the score first. I have thought about this long and hard before bringing it to you, but I can't see any other way. Who else could I possibly ask this of?"

"You're a rich woman now. Surely, we could find someone to take care of these old ghosts," John said, trying to remove himself from the task.

"We could, John, but it would just be money pulling the trigger. It needs to be more than that. It needs to be rage pulling the trigger. Yours and mine, mixed together. Their deaths need to be poetry. They need to know why they are taking their last breaths and who it is denying them their next. I want you to do the job and tell me all about it. It could be a confessional, if you like, to clear your soul after the entire job is done."

John grabbed the page again and held it up in the air. "If I do what you ask, you will be pushing me off a cliff. There is no telling what will become of me then."

"Once you complete this task, you'll be free from them forever. If you are still angry at the end and you want to add my name to the list, I will understand. But know that I will die with a clean conscience if those men are dead. That cliff you speak about has always been there for you, John. These people ..." she explained as she grabbed his hand before he could remove it again, "... put that cliff there! You have spent your life holding on to the edge of it."

John breathed out heavily. "I don't know if I can do this. I will get caught."

"Not if you are smart about it. We need your rage but a controlled rage. Learn how to make it work for you and make you smart, so you don't get caught. Let me ask you something, John. Did you recognize any of those names?"

"Yes."

"And those people you recognized ... did they hurt you or Isaac in any way when you were children?"

"Yes," John replied again, sadly.

"Then start with them. It doesn't have to be amazing. Just make them pay a price for what they did to you, and me, and even for Isaac. Did he not look after you all those years?"

"Yes."

"Then will you do it?" Susan asked, finally bringing his hand to her mouth and kissing it.

There was a weight on John's soul. Isaac had a feeling that he could have sensed it even if he were still alive.

John took a final breath and a tear rolled down his cheek. "I will try."

"Thank you," Susan sighed and started to cry too.

The Oil Slick

"Fella? Fella, are you *there*?" Isaac called wildly right after Susan and John had left the restaurant table and had gone in different directions.

As they parted, Isaac had to make a snap decision on whose orbit to anchor. He had wanted to jump to John and support him through the next stage of his processing, but it had been too long without Susan. Isaac needed some of her right now. From the look on her face, she might need him a little too. Lunch had taken its toll on all three of them.

The proposal had been stated and the mission had been accepted, but it was not the only thing on Isaac's mind.

"Yes, Isaac. I am here," Fella replied, lifting him out of Susan's orbit and into the ether.

Isaac was happy for the separation if only for a moment without the distraction of sight. "I need to understand how judgment works here. How do the Many Many judge a soul?"

"They don't, Isaac. There is no prize here. Living people make choices within their lifetimes. We are only here to witness their actions and give their lives legitimacy, not judgment. What is it that truly worries you?"

Isaac reframed the question. "Many things concern me from the conversation I just witnessed. For instance, how will Susan's soul be affected for suggesting the mission she just gave John? How will John be affected if he actually follows through and kills these people?"

"A lot of that depends on you, Isaac. Will you haunt them for these decisions? What will you whisper in their ears as they try and sleep at night? Will you congratulate Susan for coming up with the plan or torment her for condemning John with it? Every soul that arrives in this existence is greeted in the same manner regardless of what they did in their previous lifetimes. They are greeted by one much older, such as me, and they begin their process, just like you have."

"What process? You never told me that I was going through a process," Isaac said.

"As I said to you previously, Isaac, we have too many answers here. If I were to tell you all the answers upfront, they would be meaningless because you wouldn't yet have the questions."

Isaac parked his sudden frustration and instead tried to switch his brain back to Fella's logic. "You mean *context*? If you gave me all the answers upfront, I wouldn't have the context?"

"Correct."

"Okay. Here is a specific question: What is the process that I am supposedly going through?"

"You are going through the four stages of death, Isaac McGlynn," Fella replied flatly.

"And what *are* those four stages, Fella?"

"I can only tell you the first two at this point as telling you the last two may corrupt your progress. It is in the same way that forecasting a person's future may impact their life decisions, therefore changing the future they were destined for."

"I understand. What are the first two stages please?"

"Reflection and witness," Fella replied. "Reflection is the process that you were met with when you arrived here. It is a chance for a soul to reflect on their life with perspective. They see all the big moments that made them into the people they became. As you saw, it is not enough to just live through the events of a lifetime. You need to see them with perspective."

"And the second stage, Fella? Witness? Is that what I'm doing now? When do I reach the third stage?"

"Ah, Isaac ...," Fella replied in an uncomfortable way. "This is not easy to discuss in a moment. Big decisions will need to be made, but you are jumping ahead. Think for a moment. What is the *real* question you want to ask me?"

Isaac took a moment before asking the question that had been eating at him since Susan's return. He wondered if completing the four stages was something he wanted to be running *to* or running *from*. He decided that it would be a question for another day. Right now, the safety of one under his charge was at risk.

Isaac cleared his imaginary throat. There was no need to do this anymore as his voice was always perfectly clear, but the action made him feel better. "What's wrong with Susan?"

"She is starting a process of her own. You are sensing the early influence of it. She feels it also."

"What process, Fella? I don't like this."

"You and Susan are about to find out together. It is the best way. She will need you now more than ever."

* * *

The empty space disappeared, and Isaac slipped back into focus in the real world alongside Susan.

She was driving one of his prized possessions and the wildest beast from his herd. It was not the sort of car that one drove to the store for bread and milk, although on this occasion it seemed to remain complicit in its mundane task. It carried her into a car park full of cars that cost less than a single tire of this beast and came to rest about thirty-eight yards from an overused and underappreciated building.

The sign out front was digital, rendering it unreadable to Isaac, but it didn't take much guess work to know where they were. Knowing only made it worse.

Isaac followed Susan through the front door and up to the reception counter. Although the building did not inspire from the outside, the inside was different. To Isaac, it looked like it might extend itself in every direction at once. They had only walked fifteen paces from the entrance, but it already seemed like thirty.

"Can I help you?" asked one of the three maturing ladies behind the counter.

"I have an appointment with Doctor James Bennett," Susan said, looking around with a bewildered expression.

Hearing this doctor's name encouraged a blush on the receptionist's face. "Oh, sure. He's up on the third floor. You can take the elevator to your left, and then turn right when you get up there. You can't miss it."

Looking around again at the scale of the place, Isaac wasn't completely sure that the statement was correct.

Susan thanked the receptionist and walked toward the elevator.

* * *

"Fella, why are we at a hospital?" Isaac demanded.

"You must find out together, Isaac. You and Susan at the same time."

"I don't understand why you can't just *tell* me," Isaac whined, each word sounding like a petulant child who had been told to go to bed.

* * *

Susan and Isaac took the elevator to the third floor and turned right as instructed. Usually, Isaac's anchor to Susan left him feeling like they were both in a type of intimate embrace … dancing through life, with Susan taking the lead and Isaac counting one, two, three to keep step.

On this occasion, however, the intimacy was gone. Isaac couldn't put his finger on exactly what was different, but Susan was carrying more than just him around her shoulders. He was sure of it. He just didn't know what or who.

* * *

"Fella, are you following us?"

The voice came back quickly and immediately. "Yes, but we are not alone with her. And no, I can't tell you who. It is not your business to know."

"Right," Isaac said aloud but to himself. "Is it another witness like me?"

"Yes. She has you and one other watching over her."

"Okay," Isaac said. Not knowing the identity of the other

witness did not bother him. After all, it could be her mother, her grandmother, anyone except … "Fella, I just need to check. It's not her father, is it?"

"No, Isaac. You need not worry. His type is not suitable to play a role such as yours. She is watched over with love."

"Good. Thank you. Then it doesn't matter who it is."

This information told Isaac that his voice wasn't the only voice whispering in her ears. She would likely have conflicting opinions and thoughts. If so, he thought that she had done well to show herself of single mind.

* * *

When she broke her silence, Susan's voice filled Isaac's ears like melodic poetry.

"I'm Susan Melone," she said to a slightly plump receptionist. "I'm here to see Dr. Bennett."

"Melone," Isaac said to himself. "How many different names and personalities does she have?" She had always been Susan Mitchell as his assistant, and he found it unlikely that she had ever been married.

The receptionist replied, "Ah, Miss Melone. He is waiting for you. Please go in."

"Wonderful," Susan said, sailing past and barely breaking stride. If there was fear in her, it was well hidden.

The fluorescent lighting of the waiting room did nothing for her complexion, but it alone did not account for the look she was wearing. Isaac couldn't remember a time when she'd looked like this before.

A short, middle-aged doctor crossed the threshold and said, "Ah, Miss Melone. Please have a seat."

Dr. Bennett also took a seat at his desk. He could have been cast in any TV advertisement for heartburn medication. He looked her over once, but something about the situation did not allow him to enjoy the view.

Susan smiled, took a chair across from him, and allowed her spiritual entourage to settle around her. Isaac took his place immediately to her right.

"Well, let's hear it. What do you think I've got?"

"Well, you know, we really can't rush these things. I want to run a few more tests before I jump to any conclusions Susan," he answered before catching his slip of protocol. "Can I call you Susan?"

"Sure, Doc. You can use any of my names, but let's face it. You can run all those tests, and it's only going to tell you what you already know, which is …?"

The doctor's defenses crumbled instantly.

Isaac and everyone who was present leaned in like a magnifying glass finding its focus.

Dr. Bennett cleared his throat and delivered his message in one breath. "You have an aggressive form of cancer, Susan. I'm almost certain of it. I just don't know how widespread it is in your body. More tests would give me the chance to find out."

Submission

ISAAC HEARD THE SCREAM a split moment before he realized that it was his own voice. Anger, fear and betrayal delivered themselves through fire.

Susan seemed to sense the commotion and paused to allow it time to take its course.

Isaac decided to take the conversation away from her like a parent would argue away from a child. He detached himself and drifted to Fella.

* * *

"*Fella!*"

"Mr. McGlynn," Fella replied formally with just a hint of anger.

"*Fix* this!" Isaac demanded.

"I want to see you now. Face to face."

They both appeared in front of each other as they had weeks before. Fella's bodily features were still slightly out of proportion like he had been handcrafted by an amateur sculptor.

Isaac caught his breath and fought for some control. "You

need to fix this, Fella. Susan does not die like this! *Cancer!* You've got to be kidding me."

Fella's previous micro emotion had subsided, and his ocean was calm once again. "I'm sorry, but you seem to forget how we operate here, Isaac. We watch, we whisper, we give their lives legitimacy. We don't perform miracles."

"But *cancer*? Why?"

"That I can answer. It was the paint," Fella said as if it would suffice.

"What paint?"

"The paint at the orphanage. The paint that was cheaper than the rest. They finally stopped using it, but we knew it was bad for the living. We tried to stop it! We whispered and whispered, but he bought it anyway. It was cheaper."

"Toxic paint?" Isaac asked, more to himself.

"Yes … toxic. Out of the 63 children at the orphanage through those years, 21 have already died — yourself included, of course – and 17 more will die because of it."

"John too? Will *he* get this cancer?"

Fella paused in a way to suggest that he was consulting an inner search engine. "No, John was not harmed."

"Thank God," Isaac replied in relief. "He did all the same things as Susan and I did. Why is *he* safe?"

Fella spoke quickly. He knew the answer to this one himself. "It's in the design, Isaac. Some of the herd must always be stronger. Throughout time, they are the ones who fight for the tribe. When disaster strikes, they are the ones who survive and repopulate."

"*Whose* design? Who *built* all this?" Isaac asked, forever looking for an opportunity to speak directly to the man in charge.

"There is no answer that I can give you."

Isaac paused to consider the situation. "I don't want Susan to die!" he said at last. The thought traveled from his brain to his breath without corruption.

"What *we* want is not important, Isaac. We are simply here to wit…"

"No," Isaac interrupted. "I will not simply accept her death. You *must* help me fix this!"

Isaac returned himself to Susan without dismissing Fella.

"It is not for your acceptance. We have no choice," Fella said.

"Then let me talk to the Many Many. I will plead for her life."

"They already hear you through me, Isaac. There is nothing that can be done."

Isaac had never accepted his fate before, and he was not about to start in death. "I have money."

"And what price would you put on a life, Isaac?"

"For Susan, everything I have."

Fella let the words hang in the wind. They may have triggered something, or he may just be consulting the Many Many. Isaac was unsure, but he used the opportunity to witness Susan once again.

* * *

When Isaac arrived, Dr. Bennett was sitting at his desk in front of Susan and discussing her options. She could simply enjoy what was left of her short life or fight a battle she was destined to lose. It may have seemed to the doctor that she was staring absentmindedly into the distance, but Isaac knew that she was listening to everyone: the doctor, Isaac and the other soul, who was undoubtedly whispering in the wind at that very moment.

Dr. Bennett, having no consideration for the words of the dead, continued. "So, as you can see ..."

Susan put up her hand to stop him in the most elegantly respectful gesture that Isaac had ever seen. "Please. I need a moment."

The doctor nodded. "Of course, you do. This is a big decision but unfortunately one that will need to be made today." He stood up and walked around the desk, taking one of Susan's hands. "I'm truly sorry, my dear. I wish I had better news. I have to check on a few patients now. Please use my office. I will be back in thirty minutes. If you need to call anyone ..."

"No, thanks. That won't be necessary."

Dr. Bennett patted her shoulder and left the room.

Susan sat in silence for a few minutes with her head tilted slightly to the left. She was neither smiling nor frowning but instead caught in some purgatory.

After a few minutes, she took a deep breath, straightened up and said into the air, "And what about *you*, Isaac McGlynn? What would *you* have me do? Do I fight a battle I can't win, or do I simply live what's left of my life and prepare for death? This was not my plan."

The first word out of Isaac's mouth was, "Fight!"

He was about to continue but instead allowed himself an extra moment to reflect on his death. He had not fought for his life and, by the time he had heard the news of his sickness, he was told that it was already too late. Then, to counter this situation, he had greeted death on his own terms. He had simply allowed it to take him. Sure, he may have rolled with the momentum and tried to manipulate the outcome, but he had never once fought for his *health*. He had fought for life only once, and it had been in the office of Brother Anthony.

"Give me a moment," he whispered.

* * *

Isaac needed more information, so he defocused away from the living once again. "Fella?"

"Yes."

"I'm sorry about losing my temper before. It's not your fault. How do I tell her to fight when I never fought for my own life?"

"Why do you think that was, Isaac?"

Isaac considered the question deeply. "Because I had nothing to fight for."

"What about all your money, Isaac? You were a rich and powerful man."

"I know now that it was worth nothing. There was not a single thing that I needed to fight death for," he realized.

"That's why we had to end your life, Isaac McGlynn: to save your soul."

"How do we save Susan's soul without her dying?"

Fella's response was delayed, as if he were receiving instruction. "The Many Many have agreed to hear your plea for Susan's life," he said finally. "Another soul is making the same request."

"Good. Thank you, Fella," Isaac replied with a level of appreciation that he did not know he possessed. "I've been thinking. Is her mother the second witness?"

"She may be, Isaac, but I cannot tell you. It is simply another who is traveling the same path through death's stages as you are."

"How will this work? Will I see them? The Many Many?"

"No, Isaac, but they will see you. It is not possible to show you the unshowable or let you hear the unhearable. They will talk through me as we are doing now. You may go ahead and make your case," Fella added, creating a void for Isaac.

Isaac cleared a throat he didn't have and took a breath he didn't need before stepping into the light. "Firstly, thank you for hearing my plea. I don't know what words I must say to save a human life, but if there was ever a human worth saving, then Susan Mitchell is that person."

The voice that greeted Isaac was not quite Fella and not just one person. It was deeper and spoken without breath. "That is not the real name of the person you are speaking for. You are pleading for a life, and you do not even know the anointed name," the voice challenged him. "Are you sure that this person is worth saving?"

"If you are the all-knowing Many Many, then what point is a name anyway? You know *exactly* who I am talking about. May I continue?" Isaac felt as if he were staring down God himself.

"Yes."

"By giving Susan this disease, you are taking the life of an innocent. She does not deserve to die like this before she has had a chance to truly live."

"We gave her life. We lit the spark. We set her adrift into the sea of humanity, but we did not condemn her. Yet you, Isaac McGlynn ... you taught her how to die. You never once pleaded for your own life. You never shed a single tear. Now you plead for hers. Why? Why did you give up so easily?"

Isaac pondered the question. There was no point in rushing the answer. If the Many Many was all-knowing, then it certainly knew the answers to its own questions. The questions were for Isaac's benefit.

"I died because I had nothing to live for."

"You had her. You had your contract together. Anything you wanted from her was within your reach."

"No! I don't want to talk about that here."

"Why, Isaac McGlynn?"

He whispered, "Because ... I'm ... ashamed." Isaac waited for a reply but heard nothing, which he took as an invitation to continue. "I should *never* have suggested that stupid contract! I just didn't know how to love like normal people do. She is better than that, and she is worth keeping alive."

"And what exactly *is* she worth, Isaac? What is she worth to *you*?"

Isaac jumped at this question. A transaction! The one thing he had always been good at. "I HAVE MONEY!" he screamed. "I brought it with me!"

"You are not the first to bring something to heaven, Isaac McGlynn. Musicians have brought their prized instruments for centuries. We could never forcibly take from you what is yours. It must be surrendered, willingly. We never took your money. We only allowed it to be stripped from your soul. That extra rewind we granted you was not because of your money. It was your mother's rewind. She surrendered it to you and, as a result, never got to meet you before progressing to her final stage. That was her sacrifice for you. What are *you* prepared to sacrifice?"

"My mother! Is she here? Can I see her?"

"No. She has moved through the four stages of death and is beyond."

Isaac's soul ached in every direction.

"That was her sacrifice, and she accepted it willingly," the Many Many said. "We will ask you again. What are *you* prepared to sacrifice?"

"For Susan, I would sacrifice everything," Isaac said in a whisper.

In hindsight, knowing that his mother had surrendered any chance they had to talk so that he could indulge in a final rewind on the day that he met Susan felt incredibly selfish. He wished that he could have known more about the situation at the time of the request. Perhaps he would have reconsidered.

"But why, Isaac? Why *everything*?" asked the ever-persistent Many Many.

"Because I love her," Isaac admitted. He had expected this statement to be enough, but it clearly wasn't. "I didn't know it when I was alive. I only know it now."

The Many Many continued through Fella. "Love is an act of faith and submission. It is not enough for you to want to save her life. She must want it also. So far, you have done more damage to her than good. She learned how to die from you, not from us."

"Then I will teach her. I will stay at her side through the entire sickness. I will make her understand the value of a life and of love. We will fight it together. She just needs a chance to pull through, or all this is for nothing."

To Isaac, it felt like an eternity before the voice spoke again. After a long pause, they continued. "If we grant you this request, and if we give you both a chance at saving her life, it will cost you everything. If she makes it through this sickness with our help, you will never see her again. You will no longer exist in her realm. Is that understood?"

Isaac considered everything that he was being asked to sacrifice. With a resolute but heavy heart, he responded. "Yes, it is understood. Just allow me to help her through it."

"We will grant you this one last transaction, Isaac McGlynn. Everything that you have, and everything that you are, for the chance to save Susan's life. Do you submit?"

"Yes, I do. Thank you."

"Then the sacrifice is made," the Many Many said. "Return and remember that you must help her fight. If she gives up the fight, then all is lost for her life — and for you."

"What will become of me?" Isaac asked quietly.

This time, the voice was singular and back to the familiar Fella tone. "Isaac, you will enter the next stage of your death at that point."

"Which is what, Fella?"

"You will understand all when the time is right."

"Whatever it is, for her, I will pay the price."

* * *

Isaac was back in the space directly behind Susan's right ear. "You need to fight for your life, Susan!" he whispered. "We will fight for it together."

The Fight for Susan's Life

T HE NEXT THIRTY-THREE DAYS STARTED with a bang. When Susan's doctor walked back into his office after thirty minutes, concern was painted across his face. Isaac, however, was not convinced that it had been there the entire time he had been away.

"How are you coping, Susan? Do you need more time?" he asked as he rounded his desk and took his seat. If Susan did need more time, it was clear to Isaac that it would need to be somewhere else.

"No," she replied matter-of-factly. She produced a piece of paper that she had taken from Dr. Bennett's desk and had some scribbled notes. "I need you to answer a few questions before I can make a decision."

"Okay, shoot Anything."

"What happens if I do nothing?"

"You will die."

Susan seemed pleased that he had not sugar-coated his answer.

Isaac wondered if it had perhaps been a test question.

"How long would I have?" she continued.

"You would have anywhere from four months to one year, but it would not be pleasant."

"And if I chose to fight it? What is the process and what is the outlook?"

The doctor did not answer right away. When he finally did, his response was clinical and without emotion. "It all depends on how much of it has spread throughout your body. If we remove your pancreas, and if none of the cancer has spread, or we are able to contain it, you could get another five to ten years of life. If it has already spread throughout your body, it is unlikely that you will see another Christmas."

Isaac desperately looked around to try and get some sense of what date it was, but Susan answered his question.

"So less than six months?"

"Yes. But I will tell you honestly that I don't think you're riddled with cancer at this point. We can do some scans and a biopsy to be certain, but I think, in your case, we may have a chance to catch it. Of course, I can't guarantee anything until we have a look."

Susan kept the questions coming. "If I'm to survive, what chance would I have of ever having children?"

The question caught Isaac off guard. Susan had never once mentioned children to him in any context. During her lunch with John, Isaac had assumed that Susan's upbringing may have poisoned her maternal instincts in the same way that John's had.

"Well, children would be difficult. For you to get through this, your body will go through hell and back. You may recover, but I can't guarantee that your fertility would be as strong on the other side of the treatment as it is now. If that is important to you, I suggest that we remove some of your eggs and freeze them, just in case you need them later."

Isaac could see from Dr. Bennett's face that the thought of Susan having a child was secondary to her surviving the next three months.

"Then let's freeze my eggs now. How quickly can we do that before we start my actual treatment? And, before you answer, let me remind you that I am a rich woman."

The doctor's eyes betrayed him for the briefest moment at the mention of money, but he soon regained his professional composure. Isaac was sure that Susan didn't miss it.

"I need to make a call, but I'm fairly confident that we could accommodate a woman of your means and bypass the standard waiting time. Given that you have cancer, I can also ensure that you can skip the first two weeks of drugs and go straight to the hormone injections. Nine days of injections, and we can harvest the egg. The very next day, you will start your cancer treatment. There will be some extra expenses to make it all happen so quickly."

"Make it happen. And tell me, James," Susan said, breaking protocol and calling him by his first name, "should I make out the check to the hospital, to you personally or to the bookie you owe so much money to?"

Gamblers were always such easy targets. Susan had done her homework, and Isaac was proud, but pride would not shine for long on this day. Concern and fear immediately filled all available emotional air space.

Isaac knew that Susan had a chance of survival if she wanted it badly enough. This had been the condition of his deal with the Many Many. What he didn't know, however, was if Susan knew. It was nice to think that she heard his whispers and the sentiment behind them, but he could not be sure if she heard his specific words. He also didn't know if the other soul who was looking over Susan had made another deal. If so, were the two deals complementary or conflicting? Perhaps the other deal was to make Susan's death quick and painless.

Obsessive overthinking had developed a whole new meaning in heaven. Isaac's thoughts no longer followed a single thread like they had while he was alive. Instead, they now tangled like a vine climbing forever in on itself until there was simply no room left. In his tangle, Isaac had missed the doctor's answer to Susan's question about the check, but it didn't matter. One look at the doctor's face was all it took to tell Isaac that he was on the hook.

"Thank you, James," Susan said, rising to her feet.

Dr. Bennett jumped up and rounded his desk, taking Susan by the arm. "You really have taken this all very well. I would bet that you already knew much of this before coming in here."

"I think you've placed *enough* bets for now," Susan responded, not answering his question. "Anyway, it is always good to have a second opinion from a more experienced doctor."

"She knew," Isaac said to himself. "She just wanted to break it to us."

The doctor did not react to Susan. "We start tomorrow. We are not wasting any time."

* * *

When they were back in Susan's new car, Isaac resumed his

favored position behind her right ear and whispered, "You're going to beat this."

Susan giggled and drove faster than she ever had with him in the car. It took him seven minutes to realize that he didn't need to hold Susan's body to stay with her, even at this speed, so he relaxed.

Susan had not stopped giggling since she left the hospital. Isaac had never seen her full of so much energy. Sure, the oil slick — now identified as cancer — was still there, but the fire on top of it burned strong.

Over the coming days and weeks, the fire inside of Susan would temper like it was in a storm. Isaac could see it like a burning aura, bursting from and surrounding Susan. He learned to use it as a gauge to guide his care. If it burnt lower than normal, he would take the opportunity to whisper something Susan needed to hear to get her through it.

In one instance, when her fire needed a stroke during a particularly difficult chemotherapy session, Isaac reminded her about the men who had harmed her as a child. He was playing dirty, but the prize was too important to lose her because of niceties.

"If you die, are you completely sure that John will make those men pay for what they did to you? He will only do it while you are still alive. If you die, he will lose his nerve. And those men ... those men need to pay, Susan."

On that day, Isaac's words did the trick, but it only worked once.

On another occasion, when Susan was suffering the anxiety side effects of a particular drug, Isaac chimed in with the whisper, "I loved you the only way I knew how. I'm here for you. The other," he said, referring to whoever was also watching over Susan, "well, they love you also. We are both here for you, but we need you to stay there. Live for us!"

* * *

Two weeks after Susan received her prognosis, she called John and Isaac listened.

"Oh, Susan! How are you?"

"Fucking *awful*, John. GET OVER HERE!" Isaac screamed into the phone.

Susan swiped him away with her own response. "Fine, John. I've just come down with something." She may have been playing it down, but she wasn't lying completely. She had lost fifteen pounds in a week, and the command in her voice had dimmed. "What we discussed at the restaurant?" she crackled.

"Yes?" John replied wearily.

"It's important to me, John. I need to relinquish that anger, but I can't do it if you won't take it from me. It will not dissolve over time. Their punishment must come, and you are the only man still alive whom I trust."

"I know," John replied. "It's just that, for the first time in my life, I'm starting to feel normal."

"That's good, John. You are going to need an anchor point to come back to. I love you but hear this: You are *not* normal. Right now, you are a man who finds peace only when hurting others. I really wish it wasn't true. I do! I just know that, if you aren't focusing your anger on someone else, you will find a way to focus it back on yourself. I can't lose you also. I will have no one left. And who better to hurt than the guilty?

The very same people who created your anger in the first place. Make them pay for what they did to us."

"You sound like him," John replied.

"Of course, I do. I hear his voice a hundred times a day. It's like he's right next to me, for God's sake."

Isaac wondered if he had perhaps gotten too close, too attached to Susan, like a vampire feeding off the living. He pushed himself a little further out of her orbit. He wasn't sure how she did it, but she drew him back in somehow.

"Which, by the way, is a good thing," she continued. "I'm going to need him for my own little challenge."

"I think he came to me in a dream once," John added.

The three of them sat in silence for a moment, all of them casting back to moments from their memories.

John broke the silence and announced, "Yes."

"Yes *what*?"

"Don't make me say it over the phone. Yes, I will accept your anger, and I will make sure the debt is paid."

"Are you *sure*?" Susan asked, her eyes pleading into the phone. "Regardless of what may happen to me?"

"What is happening to you?" John asked, instantly concerned.

"No, nothing. I just want to make sure it gets done. It's the only way I can release it."

"You have my word."

Susan's face twitched, and Isaac noticed a single tear blaze a path down the crease of her nose and into her mouth. He would have given everything he had to wipe that tear and kiss her cheek.

"Thank you, John," Susan whispered. "I have to go now, but I'll be in touch soon. Please keep the business running for me until we talk again. I've had a little setback but nothing I can't handle."

"I will," John responded, and they both hung up.

The End of a Life or a Death

———•———

THE STRUGGLE FOR SUSAN MITCHELL's life was torturous for both her and Isaac.

For Susan, it was a combination of the traditional cancer medications and the latest experimental treatments. The pain associated with both spread throughout her body and occupied any empty space.

For Isaac, it was emotional torture. He soon learned that when you live through those you love, you die through them also. When Susan cried out in pain, he would utter a silent scream of his own, and they would join each other in a chorus of agony.

Dr. Bennett, for his part, hit her with everything he had at his disposal. His rationale seemed to be that it was best to give it to her all upfront while she was still strong enough to deal with the fallout and the side effects.

Isaac watched him closely. It was hard to see the real motivation at work in the man. Was it the money or simply the challenge that had been placed in his lap? Either way,

Isaac could tell that he was motivated for a successful outcome.

The longer the battle went on, the stronger the sense of community formed around Susan: Isaac, who rode every bump of her journey; the doctor, who had offloaded other patients to other doctors in order to spend more time with her; the other witness, whoever that was.

Isaac could sense the other soul more strongly each day like some sort of overlap he could not understand. He had even once willed it to take over from him, whispering to Susan when he had needed a break. To his astonishment, it complied. He saw nothing but, as he moved away, he could sense that his warmth and love had been replaced with another.

However, Isaac could sense one thing missing.

"You need to call John," he whispered to Susan on her twenty-third day. "This doctor cares, but he doesn't love you. You need someone alive who loves you if you are going to get through this."

Susan shook her head. Either she didn't believe that John loved her, or she didn't want to burden him with the knowledge.

Isaac would not let it rest. His job was important, but it was not enough. He would give anything to lay his hand on her forehead in her time of need, but he could not do it. "John loves you. He will help you through this. He will never forgive you if you died without telling him."

After another two days of persistence, Isaac finally found the words he needed to say for Susan to make the call. "If you die," he whispered, "you will release him from his promise and those men will go unpunished." He had tried this line once before, but this time it had a greater impact.

Susan's face changed in an instant. By that stage, all signs of life hid behind her pale, broken skin. Now, anger brought them forward like a strong gust of wind on the embers of a dying fire.

She sat upright in her hospital bed and barked at a nurse who happened to be checking on her. "My phone!"

"Do you want me to call someone for you?"

"Yes," Susan said, already out of breath. "Call John. There is only one. Tell him to come."

The nurse picked up the phone in one hand and took Susan's hand in her other. She used Susan's thumbprint to unlock the phone before scrolling through it and walking toward the door, saying, "Leave it to me."

Isaac followed her as much as he could into the outer rings of Susan's orbit, which got him to the door, but it was enough.

After a few moments, the nurse pressed the phone to her ear. "Hello. Is this John? I'm a nurse at Royal Edward Hospital. That's correct. We have a patient here named Susan, and she's asking for you."

There was a slight pause, and then she continued. "Well, actually, we have a different surname, but I'm calling you from her phone. With this lady, nothing surprises me anymore. She asked me to call you and invite you to come see her at the hospital."

There was another pause while she listened to John's response. "I had a feeling that you would not be aware," she went on. "Nobody has come to visit her. I'm so sorry to tell you, sir. She has a very advanced cancer. If you have anything to say to her, I suggest that you come quickly."

After one last pause, the nurse said, "That's correct, sir.

Royal Edward Hospital. Room 223." She looked down at the phone, but the line had gone dead.

Isaac left the nurse and returned to Susan.

John arrived at the hospital one-half hour later in a flush of anxiety and confusion. Isaac saw him rush into the room during one of Susan's vomiting attacks. The moment she looked up, John looked straight into her eyes and, for a second, he seemed to be relieved. Susan's new death mask must have thrown John into thinking that she was someone else. When he realized that it was Susan, horror found him again.

Isaac jumped across and into John's orbit. He needed a break from Susan and wanted to feel himself in John's presence again. When your entire existence is based on living in the presence of either one of two people, it becomes a celebration when both are in the same room.

"Help her, John," Isaac whispered in his ear. "She needs you!"

"Susan?" John cried. "How can that be *you*? I saw you a few weeks ago, and you weren't sick."

"*Jo-oh-n*," she said, barely able to hold the word in her grasp.

"Don't talk," he said tenderly as he rushed across the room to take hold of her body.

To Isaac, the nurse seemed relieved to have someone in the room who knew her patient.

John looked over his shoulder, through Isaac. As the nurse shuffled away, he asked, "Can you please call her doctor to come and see me? I would like to know what is wrong with her from him directly."

"Sure, sir. I'll see if I can find him."

After her latest round of dry retching, John helped Susan into a more comfortable position in the middle of her bed.

"Thank you for coming, John," Susan whispered.

John didn't answer right away. Instead, he gave her a sad smile and brushed a strand of hair from her sticky brow. "What have you done to yourself?"

Susan started to cry.

Seeing her tears now, after so much of her bravado on her part broke Isaac's heart. Had he been attached to Susan when she finally broke, he may have shattered completely.

John began to cry as well.

The look on his face told Isaac that he now knew how serious the situation was.

"The business. I need ... more ... time," she said through breaths.

"Forget that. Forget *everything*. You just worry about yourself right now."

"No!" Susan said with all the available energy at her disposal. The outburst took its toll, and she started to cough.

"You seriously want to talk about this now?" John asked.

"Not the business. Our deal," she said before coughing again.

After a few moments, Susan regained her composure. She had spoken more in the last few minutes than she had in days, and exhaustion was beginning its onslaught. She looked around the room in a blinking daze before settling her gaze directly on Isaac's position over John's right shoulder.

"Isaac, tell him," she said. She blinked twice more and passed out.

Isaac was in shock. No one alive had laid eyes on him since he passed over.

"Isaac?" John said to himself.

At that moment, the doctor came in to greet John. "Is she out?"

John returned his gaze to Susan to be sure. "It looks like it. I think she may have been delirious."

"No surprise there. I have her on three treatments at once."

"Is that safe?"

"No, not normally," Dr. Bennett said, "but this is no normal woman. We are not even sure that we know her real name. Perhaps you can help us. Every time we get a piece of information on her, it comes wrapped in a different name. We only know her by DNA at this point. Anyway, let her rest. Come to my office, and we can talk there."

"Susan," John said, reaching across and pulling the blankets up over her shoulders. "Her name is Susan. The rest doesn't matter." He kissed her on the forehead, and the two men left the room.

* * *

Isaac waited until John got to the door before jumping back to Susan. He already knew everything that John was about to hear. He would have traded anything to be able to do the simple act of pulling the blanket over her shoulders, as John had just done so effortlessly, or place a hand in comfort at any time over the past month. Unfortunately, physical comfort was only for the living. Instead, Isaac had suffered the horror of watching the one he loved shiver through the nights. For the moment, Isaac allowed himself to enjoy the warmth he was sure that she was getting.

After seventeen minutes of sleep, Susan sputtered back to life through a series of violent coughs that forced her awake. At first, her eyes rolled in their sockets like a slot machine about to finalize its draw. Then, and to Isaac's complete surprise, she found him.

Isaac performed a rotation to check the likely scenario behind him, but there was none.

Susan's eyes stared directly at him, but her face did not change. If she saw him, she was not giving it away, but she was not looking away either.

Isaac rotated three feet to her right, which was within her orbit.

Susan's eyes followed, overextended and then rectified their gaze on Isaac again like a seasick drunk. As before, her head and mouth did not move. She was a perfect Mona Lisa, her faced carved in stone with piercing eyes forever following the observer.

"Susan?" Isaac whispered. "Can you see me?" He didn't yet allow himself to get excited by the prospect.

Susan didn't shift. For the eternity of seven whole seconds, she said nothing.

"Susan, it's me," Isaac said, raising his voice. He tried to wave his arms, but it had been so long since he had needed them that he wasn't sure if he still had them.

Susan blinked and mumbled the word, "Isaac."

Isaac brought himself right up to her space and screamed, "YES!"

Susan crunched her eyes tightly in much discomfort.

Isaac, who would regret it later, exploded in a flurry of words. "Oh, my God! I can't believe that you can *see* me!"

"Stop … please!" Susan said behind her closed eyes.

Isaac stopped himself immediately.

"I can see you, Isaac, but I can't hear you. Whatever you did just now, please stop. It hurts too much."

Isaac pushed himself further away from her, to the edges of her orbit, and whispered, "Susan, can you hear me *now*?"

Susan said nothing but managed to reopen her eyes and find him once again. The discomfort across her face was taking its leave. She watched him again.

"Susan?"

"I can see you, Isaac, but I can't hear you. Not like I did before," she said, exhaling slowly.

* * *

Isaac whispered over his shoulder, not wanting to hurt her further, and asked, "Fella, how can she see me?"

Fella's voice came right away as if he had also been watching the entire event. "She is closer to death than she was before."

It wasn't the answer that Isaac was hoping for. "Then why can't she *hear* me?"

"Because she is closer to you than you are to her."

Before processing the answer, Isaac turned his attention to Susan to make sure that this conversation was not hurting her. When he was sure that it wasn't, he said, "That doesn't make any sense, Fella."

"Then ask the right question, Isaac. I have all the answers."

"Okay. How do I talk to her so that doesn't hurt her?"

"You can't have it both ways, Isaac. Let her see you. Let it bring comfort."

"She needs to live, Fella."

"You made the deal. You sacrificed all for her, but the decision to live or die is still hers, just like it was yours, even if she doesn't know it."

It was another answer that left Isaac feeling unsatisfied. "Then what does she see? When she looks at me now, what does she see?"

"Only she can see through her eyes, Isaac."

* * *

A foreign voice caught Isaac off guard as he was preparing his next question for Fella.

"Ah, you are awake," the voice said with its body walking straight through Isaac's vantage point as if he didn't exist. He usually did not enjoy this sensation, but at this important moment it felt particularly humiliating.

Susan tried to recover him in her vision without success. Isaac was lost in the crowd of the living.

Dr. Bennett and John spread themselves out around her bed, one on each side, forming a perfect living triangle. John took her right hand in his and placed his other hand on her shoulder. After a quick performance smile, the doctor read her vitals and studied all the information on it like a chess master preparing for his next thrust into the game.

"How do you feel?"

Susan groaned. "I feel like death itself is watching over me," she said. She flashed a quick look about the room.

It seemed to Isaac that he was not in her normal vision, but she was learning to focus on him when needed.

The doctor was ready to discuss his final move. "Susan, I know that you would not want me to mince my words, so

I'm not going to. Right now, you are drifting. Buying time but not winning. You could say that you are going downhill slowly. This is not healing. It is just prolonging life. The problem is that the longer this goes on, the weaker you will become. If we don't do something big soon, all of your opportunities to stay alive will have passed us. Do you understand what I'm saying to you?"

"Yes."

"I have one option left. But, if we do this last procedure, it will involve putting you into a medically induced coma, which you may not survive. This step could be saying good-bye for good."

Saying Goodbye

"Can you please tell us more about what you are proposing, so we have all the facts?" John asked.

"Sure," Dr. Bennett said, turning back to Susan. "We will be trying a technique called 'adoptive cell transfer.' We have removed part of the cancer from your body already. From that, we were able to determine some of the friendly T cells within it. With a little time, during the past few weeks, and with all the money in the world — which Susan seems to have — we were able to cultivate it. We have an army of billions of these great T cells now, which we would inject back into her body. Basically, turbocharging her immune system."

"Perfect! Why haven't you done this already?" John replied.

Susan looked at the doctor.

"We weren't sure if we could cultivate enough cells in time, and we were concerned that Susan might already be too far gone to cope with this treatment."

"And?" John asked, and Isaac echoed silently.

"And we still aren't sure. We could use double what we have, and it might be for no good anyway. But ... that's not the worst of it. If we were to try this — if we put Susan in a coma — I can't guarantee that she will ever wake up. It could be eyes open for a few weeks until she wastes out, or a coma tomorrow and that is it. She never wakes up."

"Or a coma, and then she pulls through?" John asked.

"That's what we would hope for, yes."

"I see. Susan, do you understand what was just said?" Susan nodded.

"You know her best, John. I will need you to vouch for her ability to make this decision in her current condition."

It was clear to Isaac that the doctor's preference was to keep fighting the disease. He was a master of his craft and had a lot of money on the line.

John found Susan's gaze and held it. He was searching her for the fight that may be left within her bones.

Isaac took the opportunity to jump across to John's orbit. Given that both orbits were overlapping, it was more a token gesture, but it did give him access to John's ear.

"Susan would want to fight, John, and not drown in cancer. Give her this last fight," he whispered in John's right ear.

John kissed Susan on the forehead. "Are you ready for this fight? Or do we just get you a little more comfortable and prolong it?"

Susan allowed herself a moment to reconsider. "I need ... to talk ... to you alone first."

"Of course," the doctor said before turning to the door. "I'll give you both some time."

John reached for Susan's hand and held it in his. Isaac could feel it in his own way through John. They both held her hand in silence for the next two minutes.

"Our deal ..." Susan started, her voice a little clearer than earlier. "Our deal still stands regardless of what happens to me?"

"Just worry about your health now, Susan."

"No!" Susan spat through the pain. "You *promised* me. I gave you the names. Each of them needs to pay for what they did to me. You are the only one I have left."

"Tell her no," Isaac whispered into John's ear. "If she dies, the deal is off."

John must have been considering the same leverage. "Susan, if you die, I'm not sure that I could kill those men. If you go, I have nothing left. I was barely holding on before you came back to me. Without you around, I don't know what I will have left."

"Coward! You promised me that you would make them pay," Susan said through anger and a stain of disappointment.

"She is scared, John. Hold your ground," Isaac whispered. "You need to keep her alive. Right now, that comes before everything, including the truth."

"Isaac … ENOUGH!" Susan screamed. "Get out of his head. Let him be a man and stand on his own two feet."

Isaac pulled back into their outer orbit, giving them both space. This was a decision for the living.

"I can sense him here with us too," John said. "But it wouldn't matter what he said. My answer is still my answer. If you fight this and win, I swear to you that I will make those men pay for what they did to you. But if you choose to die, or don't fight it with everything you've got, I can't guarantee that I won't be far behind you. Being involved with the business is great, but there is nothing left here for me if you go. I never cared about the money."

Once again, the three of them sat in silence.

"Then I have no option. I need to live for both of us and for the death of the others. You have been unfair to me today, John. We had a deal, and you changed it," Susan said.

"Life is unfair, Susan."

"You can tell the doctor to start his preparations."

John kissed her forehead once again and left the room.

Isaac jumped back to Susan and covered her with as much of his spirit as he could.

"You just gave up on us, Isaac, and now you expect me to fight through all this pain?" Susan asked the air before starting another coughing fit. "You … demand too much of your people."

"I'm sorry, Susan," Isaac whispered.

* * *

Dr. Bennett came back to the room 30 minutes later to check Susan's vitals against her chart.

"Susan, John tells me that you are okay to go ahead with the final treatment?"

Susan let out a labored exhale. "Yes."

"Good! Then we start tomorrow."

"Tomorrow, I'll be one day weaker. Can you start today?"

"I can, but I thought that you might like a day to say your goodbyes and get any paperwork in order," he said sheepishly.

"I've already arranged for you to be paid the money we agreed," said Susan, cutting to the chase. "As for goodbyes, the only people I care about in this world are either dead or buying a bag of chips from the vending machine outside."

"I can be ready to go within the hour."

"Good. Make it happen."

* * *

It was more than an hour, but not much more. Isaac watched as Susan's body was needled and prodded into position for the surgery. A syringe, which looked like it should be used for livestock, was thrust into her veins and its contents voided unceremoniously.

John had assured Susan that she would be fine, but it was clear to Isaac — and likely Susan — that he had his concerns. He was potentially saying goodbye to the only other person in the world he cared for.

"We are going to need you to wait outside for the next 30 minutes or so, Mr. Hannebery," said the most senior nurse. "We'll call you as soon as it's clear for you to come back in."

As John left the room, Dr. Bennett started his work. "Susan, count backwards from 10."

Susan's eyes flickered. Fear was igniting her expressions in ways that Isaac had never seen before, but she allowed herself one last rebellion. "Ten, nine," she coughed, "eight …" and then her light was out.

* * *

"Fella, are you there?" Isaac whispered over his shoulder. The seriousness of the moment seemed to call for a whisper.

"I am always here, Isaac."

"I want to talk to her."

"We anticipated this request, Isaac. It has been discussed."

"I have nothing left to offer you. You already have my money and my soul."

"That is the great secret, Isaac. A soul can be given more

than once. Just like the cells in a physical body can die and regenerate. You are not the soul you were yesterday, and you will be different again tomorrow. Love is the giving of the soul again and again, regardless of which side of the great divide you may be on."

"I think I understand," Isaac said, shifting his priorities. "You mentioned that there was debate around me talking to Susan?"

"Yes. Some argue that you had your chance to tell her everything while you were alive, and you told her nothing. They say that they granted you an exception for John already and you don't deserve another."

"What do *you* say, Fella?"

"Isaac, I fight for you. I have arranged passage for you to say your last words to Susan. It has become my sacrifice for you."

"Thank you, Fella," Isaac said, relief washing over him like a warm wave. "Before I go, can I ask you why? Why do this sacrifice for me?"

"My price is that you will never know who I am. And, without you or anyone alive knowing my name, I will die the second death. I will move on from this plane to the next, which is okay. I am ready. I will miss you though, Isaac McGlynn." Fella allowed himself a moment before continuing. "It is a fair price, and I pay it gladly."

"I understand," Isaac said. "From the bottom of my heart … thank you!"

"I will send you to her now. We will speak only once again after this, so be ready when the time comes."

"Only once more?" Isaac started to say, but the connection went dead. The world around him and the hospital exploded into midnight black.

* * *

After a few moments, color started to bleed into the darkness like a slow swirl of paint eventually landing on a canvas. Piece by colorful piece, the world around him rendered itself into view.

"Here again?" Isaac asked himself. "Why does everything always come back to the orphanage?"

Susan was back in Brother Anthony's office — the same place that Isaac had killed him. She was hiding behind a filing cabinet. "Isaac?" she asked in her tiny voice from years ago. "Are you in my dream?"

"Yes, Susan. I am here."

"Good," she replied as if his presence alone was enough.

"Why here, Susan? Of all the places you could go in your dreams, why come here?"

"A part of me has always been here, Isaac. I faced death three times in this very room before I was even 10 years old. I guess it makes sense that I would come back here to die."

"This time is different, Susan," he said, imploring her to reconsider.

"Why? Death is death."

"Because, this time, your survival is your choice."

"And what do I have to go back to? My rage? It doesn't seem to possess me here like it does back there. I know it's waiting for me like a rabid dog. I'm ashamed of what I've asked John to do for me on its behalf."

"Then don't go back for rage. Go back for love."

Susan almost suppressed a scoff but not completely. "*Love?* What do *I* know about love? We were all broken people, Isaac. Who will love me?"

"I love you, Susan."

"But you died! *Remember?* You didn't love me enough to stay alive."

"I think I *did* love you in the only way I knew how, which I know was a terrible substitute."

"I don't know how," Susan replied quickly.

"You have time to learn. Let the rage run its course and exhaust itself. Let John complete his mission, and then you can find yourself love when you finally have room for it."

"But John? What will happen to him if he carries out my wishes? I am so angry with those men that I'm saying things to John that I'm not sure I even believe."

"I'll help John," Isaac said. "It's what I have done my whole life. Without even meaning to, you've already saved him from himself once. It's my turn now. His rage needs to run its course as well. If he can't do it, I will do everything in my power to pull him out of the obligation. I'm not sure if he will ever find love for himself, but he has you, and he will do anything for you now."

"What if I wake up and forget everything?" Susan's question hung in the air for a few more moments, and then she finally stood up.

The room around them dissolved from focus, but a shadow of its outline remained. The light in the room started to dim, and the walls began to fade.

"Susan, what if you don't wake up? That is the question that worries me much more. I think my time with you is almost done. Please go back. No matter how bad life is, death is worse. And, as much as I want you with me, I would rather never see you again, knowing that you are alive and happy, than have you here." The world around Isaac collapsed, and his link with Susan was almost broken as he said, "Please, Susan, forgive me! I love you."

Isaac's world went midnight black.

* * *

After two days in a coma, Susan awoke and knew two things for sure: She had broken the back of her cancer and Isaac was no longer with her. He was not silent or elsewhere. Her link was gone.

At that moment of realization, she cried for his death.

The Four Stages
of Death

———•———

ISAAC RETURNED FROM SUSAN'S DREAM but not to the real
world. Instead, he was in the staging world where he had
first met and named Fella. Surrounded by white, but not so
overwhelming that he had to squint, it had the essence of a
space created for a specific occasion.

"A heavenly meeting room," he thought.

Fella materialized in front of him in the same form he'd
used previously, with all the human parts but not the right
dimensions.

"You don't need to take human form for me, Fella," Isaac
said. "Just be yourself."

The elasticity in the air around Fella dissolved, and he
appeared instead as sparkling energy without a source.

"Thank you, Isaac. It had been so long. I was sure I that
was getting it wrong!"

"Will I see Susan again?"

"No."

"Does she live?"

"Yes."

Isaac let out a sigh. "Will she remember our conversation?"

"Who can know what is in the mind of the living, Isaac? We only observe their actions."

"And I won't see you again after this, Fella?"

"Our time together is finished. You will be on your own from here."

Isaac paused at the sadness of Fella's statement. He was about to lose the only friend he had in the afterlife.

"Fella, one lifetime is not enough."

"You never learned to master the art of living, Isaac."

"Then let me try again, please. Give me another chance to get it right."

"Not yet, Isaac. You are close, but you have not yet progressed through the four stages of death." Fella's energy burned a little brighter with each word, and then pulsed back to normal.

"What *are* the four stages of death, Fella?" Isaac asked finally.

There was silence before the answer, which suggested that Fella was seeking approval.

"The four stages of death are the stages through which a soul must progress before it can regenerate," Fella finally said. "I started to explain this to you once before, but I will start again so you understand."

"Stage one," he continued, "is reflection. Reflection is the process you began with when you arrived here. It is a chance for a soul to reflect on their own life with perspective. They see all the big moments that made them into the people they became. As you saw, it is not enough to just live through the events of a lifetime. You need to see them with perspective."

"I understand."

"Stage two is witness. We must play our part in validating the living, and they play their part in validating us. In the same way that you have been witnessing Susan's life, she has been living to validate your existence. An actor without an audience does not exist, and neither does the audience. Do you understand?"

"Yes, I get it," Isaac replied. "What's the third stage?"

"The third stage of death is submission," Fella answered. "Submission is the act of sacrifice. In the same way you have sacrificed for Susan and John, others have sacrificed for you, including myself. Sacrifice is the currency of love."

"And the fourth stage, Fella? What's the fourth stage of death?"

"The fourth stage is reassignment. Once a soul is ready, it is considered for reassignment. At this point, a soul is evaluated and appraised for its next mission, which may include another lifetime or a promotion to the upper levels. We have called these upper levels the Many Many, but they are not the top of the tree — only the next branch."

"What are they, Fella? What do they do other than provide answers to my questions?"

"They are the answers to your questions, Isaac, in a way that I will never be able to explain. They are the fabric that we all live under. They are existence for all."

"I don't want that, Fella. Not yet. I want to live again, and this time I want to feel love. *Real* love. Not just two naked bodies fighting each other for release, but the love of a mother, a father and a partner."

"You have sacrificed a lot, Isaac, but you have not yet sacrificed all. You are not yet ready to go back," Fella replied with a touch of sadness around the edges of his voice.

"Then what will become of me from here?"

"John," Fella replied. "John's story is about to be told, and you need to help him tell it. He will need you in ways that neither of you can yet comprehend. You will need to take him to the edge and bring him back again. Without each other, you are both lost. It has always been the case for you two. Your fates are aligned."

"Half the time he doesn't even know that I'm here."

"He will," Fella replied.

"Great. So the next chapter of my death will be entitled, 'The Hit Man and His Guardian Angel,'" Isaac said sarcastically.

"No, Isaac. You will hear the final confession of John Hannebery." Fella paused again, waiting for instructions from the Many Many. "Isaac, I have said too much but also maybe just enough. Our time together is coming to an end. I am honored to have been the witness to your death."

"Fella, before you go, I have one last question."

"Yes?"

"If we've been helping the living over all of time, and they've been helping the dead, why isn't it already perfect?"

"Because life's struggle is its trophy, Isaac. You will learn this more the next time around."

Isaac's world went midnight black. Once again, he waited for a light to shine in the darkness.

THE END

About the Author

Andrew Hood was born in Victoria, Australia, in 1973 and is an author, a blogger, an IT sales director, and a family man.

His personal blog, *The Weekly Tipping Point*, was awarded No. 39 in the "Top 101 Best & Most Inspiring Blogs." Since 2014, he has been a guest blogger on *The Guided Mind* and *Change Your Thoughts — Change Your Life*.

Since then, he has published his debut novella, *Suggesting Murder*, and his first nonfiction book, *Leadership Secrets from the Greatest Leaders of all Time*.

Interview with the Author: Andrew Hood

What is *The Man Who Corrupted Heaven* really about?

This book will have a different meaning for anyone who reads it. For me, it is a book about perspective. It is about how we see our lives from our perspective and how limiting this can sometimes be.

The main character of this book, Isaac McGlynn, was extremely rich and successful, albeit from a fractured background. However, he soon learns that, within one small step away from his life — a different perspective — everything he believed to be true was not. It was simply his perspective of his world that made it true for him.

In writing this book, I encourage the reader to occasionally try and get a glimpse outside of their perspective ... if that's even possible!

Where do you get your ideas from?

Like a lot of books, this one started from a simple question and grew from there. A few years ago, I heard a famous quote:

"You can't take anything with you when you die." This got me thinking, "Why not?" and "What if that wasn't true?"

After obsessing over these questions for about half an hour, I wrote the first two lines of my book: "It is often said that you come into this world with nothing and leave it the same way. Isaac McGlynn, however, was determined to prove this adage wrong."

Then I wrote the title, *The Man Who Corrupted Heaven.*

At that point, I had no idea what the book was about, but that's where it all started.

In the book, your version of heaven is not the typical Christian version. Is this the heaven you believe in?

I guess this version of heaven is one that I can live with without too much inner turmoil. For me, I think it works somehow. It is a practical version of heaven with a hierarchy.

There is a story behind your character names? Where do you get your character names from?

I needed to find a system because I'm not good at making them up from scratch like some authors. I got the names from my favorite Australian football team — the Sydney Swans — and mixed the first and last names of different players. I use the Netball team sheet for the women. It helps because I feel like I know them just a little already before they even hit the page.

Who are your writing influences?

There are so many amazing authors out there, but there are three who get my money, no questions asked, the moment they launch a new book.

One is Paulo Coelho, the author of *The Alchemist* and so many other great books. His writing is so simple to read, and he packs such a big philosophical punch in each of his books that I can't say no. Reading his books reminds me that a great book can teach you a lot about yourself, even though it was written by someone else.

Another is Mitch Albom, the author of *The Five People You Meet in Heaven*. Again, small books with a massive punch. I love his depth and simplistic writing style, which I have tried to make my own for this book.

Finally, Carlos Ruiz Zafón, the author of *The Shadow of the Wind*. He is a Spanish novelist who is very unlike the other two guys. His books are much larger and can be difficult to read at the start, but once he has you in his grip, his stories are fantastic. I love the magic he brings into the world, like his concept of the "cemetery of forgotten books."

All these guys have had a massive effect on my life and on my writing.

Is there a sequel in the works?

Unlike many other writers, I was not born to write stories. For me, it is simply the best way to organize and create my thoughts and share them with people I care about. Because of this, you are unlikely to ever see a series of 10 books with the same characters, no matter how lucrative that market can be. I am just not built to turn out hundreds of action stories or romance novels.

Having said that, however, I am not quite finished with these characters just yet! Here's a brief overview of what is to come in this series of three books. The current working title of the sequel is *The Final Confession of John Hannebery*. While this book has been a study of perspective, the next one will be about anger. The final book in the series — Susan's book — will be about control. Perspective, anger and control.

At this point, I am planning to write 10 books, so I will need to make sure that everyone is amazing because you all deserve the best I have to offer.

Do you have any final words for your readers?

Again, thank you, thank you, thank you! For reading my words, even if you disagree with them. For being my witness. For seeing my tree fall in the woods! (I hope this reference isn't too obscure. You will get it if you read the book.)

Without you reading this book, I am no author. I will always remember and respect that fact, regardless of whether I sell a hundred books or a million.

My warmest regards,

Andrew

Coming
Soon

The Man Who Settled the Score
/
The Final Confession of John Hannabery

By Andrew Hood

CHAPTER ONE

"Forgive me father, for I have sinned...

That's what they say isn't it? They do on TV anyway.

They then say something like – My last confession was a year ago, only that is not exactly true. For me it was at least thirty years ago, when I was four. You see, as a child I was forced to confess, a lot. I even confessed to things I didn't do or understand.

Can you be forgiven for something that you don't understand and you're quite sure you didn't do in the first place?

I doubt it, but I was told what to say and I said it, through gritted teeth and a swollen eye.

In fact, scratch that question, it's better if I do all the talking. I will never have the strength, nor the time, to get through this entire confession if I must stop and ask you questions or even worse, wait for you to answer them.

No Father, for now just sit back and take this all in. You have been kind enough to give me this time and now I intend to take full advantage of it. I have never been a selfish man but today I'm going to indulge myself, just a little, because at the end of the day this is what this experience is supposed to be about. I get a few things off my chest, I'm forgiven, and we all go about our lives as if everything is okay.

You are a lucky man though. This will be my final confession and you have the front row seat at this show.

Ahhhh.... 'My final confession' I like the sound of that. It rolls off the tongue like a magic carpet defying gravity for the first time. It also breaks the bond between the old and the new. Even hearing myself talking to you like this makes me feel a little smarter than usual. I think I'm going to like this new me!

Oh, and I know that it is not usually customary, but I am going to tell you my name. Are you ready? Good, here it is – John Hannebery.

I wonder how many of the sinners that have sat in this confession box have had the courage to disclose their own names. They must sit here and slowly bleed their pathetic sins, their masturbations, their dirty thoughts, their adultery, and yet how many would have the courage to use their own name?

Me, as you can probably tell already, I'm a little different than most. I don't live in fear anymore, that all stopped for me when I was a child. If we get time, we can talk about that later but I'm still unsure if my little confession will take that path. I'm making it up as I go along you see.

I think that it is important to note also, if this confession is to work, that I don't care what you think of me, or almost anyone else for that matter. I invite you to judge me. Take my little story to heart and cast your stones if you will. It won't bother me a bit. Seriously! Why? Well when you have pointed a gun at your own head as many times as I have without pulling the trigger you start to laugh when others try to do the same.

No, in my entire adult life there have only ever been two people that I have cared anything about. One was my brother Isaac, who is now dead, and the other is our Susan. She almost died from cancer eight months ago. They say she has five years left at most and then she'll be gone too. Personally, I think death will need all of that five years to recover from the last fight it picked with her. When it comes after her next time it had better be ready.

Strange that I called her 'our Susan' just now. I only really found her a year ago and she was always Isaacs girl but right now she and I are all each other has left. I guess that's another story.

So, where was I? Oh yes, judge away!

As I tell this little story there will be some things that I may share with you from my background, a little insight here and there, and others that you will just need to judge me for by my actions. After all isn't it our actions that define us not our history? To society I am a killer, they don't care what was done to me as a child. And rightly so, I guess. When I am gone, my actions and this confession will be the only validation of who I ever was.

There I go getting all philosophical again. This is not the usual me. This process is bringing out a whole new side to my personality.

No, I need to stop it. I don't want to misrepresent myself. I am a thug, a killer, a man who likes to hear people break. It is all I have ever been within the confines of this world. I don't feel sympathy for any of the victims I have damaged because I didn't make the decision, I simply follow orders. Does a dentist's drill feel sorry for the tooth? No, it simply carries out the dentists' command and bores the hole.

That's me, the drill, the hammer, the instrument. The moment that it gets personal for me, all is lost. I will touch on why a little later in my story.

I want you to know that I'm not completely heartless though. No women or children were harmed in the creation of this story, and never an innocent. No, the people I went after had it coming. I'm not saying that women can't be bad, I have just never been sufficiently damaged enough to harbor enough hatred toward them. But men, they can be real motherfuckers.

Whoops, sorry, probably shouldn't have said that in here, a church of all places. I will try to keep the swearing to the barest minimum from here on out.

The titles 'hitman' or 'killer' are still quite new strings to my bow. It started only twelve months ago, and I still get a little embarrassed whenever I introduce myself as such. I wonder if there needs to be a certain amount of death before you qualify for the titles, or will just one or two deaths do? If I get time, I will need to look that one up. Don't worry though, I more than qualify at nine but that little question always stuck in my head. At what point do you qualify?

I keep getting distracted, that will need to stop now if we are to get through this.

Firstly, let me ask you a rhetorical question. What do you give a man who has everything?

The answer – a gun, a list, and a mission.

So that is where we will start."

Made in United States
North Haven, CT
06 December 2022

27977909R00153